THE SEA CAPTAIN'S REDEMPTION

THE DIMARCO EMPIRE

CINDY REDDING

Copyright © 2023 by Cindy Redding

All rights reserved.

This book contains adult language and scenes. This story is meant only for adults.

This is a work of fiction. Names, places, characters, and incidences are a product of the author's imagination. Any resemblance to persons, living or dead, organizations, events or locales is entirely coincidental.

No part of this book may be reproduced in any form or by any electronic or mechanical means, including information storage and retrieval systems, without written permission from the author, except for the use of brief quotations in a book review.

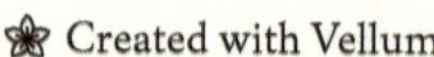 Created with Vellum

OVERVIEW

Free spirited cruise ship captain, Lorenzo DiMarco never wanted love. All he needed was his women in each port to satisfy his unconventional needs. Until…Francesca Russo, his best friend's younger sister came aboard his ship for a two week Hawaiian cruise.

The fun loving innocent opens Lorenzo to a new world of emotions he never knew he needed. Can Lorenzo change his ways for the blue eyed beauty? Can the sea captain get his redemption?

For my beautiful daughters, Heather and Jennifer
To new beginnings filled with adventure, happiness and love.

CHAPTER 1

*L*orenzo DiMarco flung his white, gold-braided hat across the luxury hotel's bedroom. A smile on lips that he'd been told by numerous women were seductive at the very least. Today only two sleek naked women lay across the king-size bed, waiting for him. For the past ten years, all he wanted or needed was uncomplicated, uncommitted sex. The kind of sex he would indulge in now. Both women wanted the same, with no commitments. Ever.

Elana, the blond beauty, sat up and caught his captain's hat, placing it jauntily on her head. She laughed. "I won. So, you do what I say," she spoke in her native Spanish.

"Yes, my beauty. Whatever you want," he growled.

Carmen flipped her brunette locks over her shoulder and pouted her sexy, red-painted lips. "She caught your hat last time. No fair, Lorenzo. I've been waiting too long." She parted her shapely legs and rubbed her shaved pussy. She spread her seam and exposed her glistening folds. "See how much I need you." Both women shaved their pussies, painted their nails red, and wore red lipstick for him. Just the way he liked it.

"*Bellissima,* you'll have to wait your turn," he said, tugging his shirt off and unzipping his pants. "I promise to make you come first, so be patient for me."

"Oh yes, I'll wait." She clapped her hands together, smiling at him.

He stripped out of his uniform, walking over to the bed, holding his erection. "Today, I don't have much time. I have to be back on board the ship sooner than usual and since you both have red lipstick on, why don't you suck my dick first?" He reclined against the taupe colored upholstered headboard in the center of the bed. Lorenzo folded his hands behind his head, spreading his legs. The two luscious women scrambled to kneel on either side of his six-foot two-inch athletic frame.

Passing a couple of hours with these two beauties would take the edge off his throbbing need. He loved the feel of both their tongues licking his dick, his balls. *Ahh, so good when the blonde took him fully into her mouth.* The head of his dick slipped down her throat, and the brunette continued to lick and kiss his balls.

He had to stop them, or it would be over too soon. Lorenzo nudged the brunette. "Carmen, ride me." His voice was gruff. "I promised you would come first."

She eagerly straddled him before slowly lowering herself down his shaft. Elena's sweet tongue continued to lick his balls. Lorenzo held Carmen to steady her as she played with her nipple rings while she rode him. Once she orgasmed, Elena took her place riding him, opening herself so he could rub her clit. When she screamed her pleasure, she moved to his side. Both women kissed and licked his dick, running their tongues on the ridge under his engorged head.

"That's it. Oh *si, si,* just like that." He exploded, releasing all his tension, coming on their breasts, until Carmen took him into her mouth, greedily swallowing the last bursts of his come. Elena lay on one side of him, kissing his chest, while Carmen stroked him with her tongue, keeping him in her mouth. Gradually, his breathing returned to normal. He lay there for a moment, sliding his fingers through both women's long hair. "Ah my beauties, you always make my return to this port special." He sat up.

"Do you have to go already?" Elena said.

"You won't be back for two weeks. Isn't this your Hawaii run?" Carmen added.

"Yes, my beauties. You know my schedule so well." Lorenzo tucked his shirt into his pants, then went back to the bed to kiss both women. At the door, he said, "Listen for the sound of the ship's horn at four o'clock. I'll be thinking of both of you."

He strode to the elevator, whistling a tune. It was a short walk from the five-star hotel to the pier where his ship, *Diamond of the Seas*, had docked before dawn this morning. It was turnaround day, and he needed to be back on board earlier than usual. His best friend Gus Russo's baby sister, Francesca Russo, would be a guest for the sixteen-day specialty cruise. Round-trip from San Diego to Hawaii, then a stop in Ensenada, Mexico and back to San Diego.

He smiled, remembering how Francesca would follow her brother Gus, him and his cousin, Giorgio Lombardo, all over Palermo. Gus would shoo her back home to his parents. Her bottom lip would quiver, and Lorenzo usually bought her a gelato.

"Here, to make you feel better," he'd say in their Sicilian dialect before she wiped her tears and ran home. She was ten, with the cutest blond pigtails and big blue eyes. That was the last time he saw her, ten years ago when he left Sicily, vowing never to return.

It was almost zero hour. The hour when the last of the passengers departed the ship before the next group of passengers boarded. Turnaround day was one of the busiest days for the crew. Not only taking on new passengers, but fuel and food, enough for the sixteen days plus another two weeks, just in case.

The dock was busy with activity as he boarded through the crew entrance near the bow of the ship. His crew and security officers came to attention when they recognized him. Taking the private officer's elevator up to the bridge deck, he walked the few feet to his cabin. He reminded his personal steward Mario to let him know the minute Ms. Russo would be ready to come aboard. He showered off the fragrance of his two favorite women—well, his favorite women—in this port.

FRANCESCA RUSSO COLLECTED her bags from the airline carousel, cleared U.S. Customs and Immigration, then boarded the complimentary transfer bus for the ride to the San Diego pier. She was too excited to be exhausted from the long flight and finally on her way to the *Diamond of the Seas* cruise ship. Too bad her BFF Stella had to miss out on this trip after breaking her femur bone; she'd been in traction and had surgery. Stella was recovering, which prevented her from flying. Francesca didn't want to go without her best friend, but Stella insisted she go and have enough fun for both of them.

Francesca couldn't wait to see Captain DiMarco. The last time she set eyes on the handsome hunk was ten years ago when she was ten and he twenty-two. Her brother Gus was friends with Lorenzo DiMarco and Giorgio Lombardo. Both Lorenzo and Giorgio were so unbelievably handsome, but Lorenzo made her heart skip a beat whenever he was around. She'd had such a crush on him back then.

Daydreaming about him and drawing hearts with their initials in it—normal kid things.

Francesca's parents were relieved that at least Gus's friend would be there. Someone she knew to keep an eye on her. She was embarrassed by that; she was old enough to travel and have an adventure by herself. *What did they think?*

A smile lifted the corners of her lips, thinking of Lorenzo. While scrolling on the Contessa Lines website under the section, Meet Our Captains, she saw a photo of him. He was definitely handsome with chiseled features, jet-black hair, and those black-as-night eyes. Francesca leaned her head back against the bus seat. *If anything, now, I may want him to do more than watch me. After all, I'm an adult.*

Francesca slipped her phone from her bag and snapped some photos. Excitement buzzed through her when she saw the famous burger place. She was so happy to have this time off before she began her career in fashion design. She and Stella planned on opening a boutique where they would sell her designs. Stella would manage the store and do most of the sewing, while she would make the designs. Francesca made most of the outfits she brought on the trip. She took a selfie just before the bus parked at the Embarcadero. She typed: **And so, it begins! My American Adventure,** and posted it to her Instagram.

Francesca stepped off the bus on the pier. The *Diamond of the Seas* looked majestic docked with long, thick ropes holding her in place. People milling about, some walking along the pier snapping photos. Others walked in front of baggage stewards while they pulled their luggage on carts. Some travelers pushed baby carriages, and others carried their bags. She was eager to begin this new experience. A man in a white shirt and white pants stepped up to her. "Ms. Russo?" he said in Italian.

"*Sì.*"

"I'm Mario Luna—Captain DiMarco's steward, and I'm here to help you board and take you to Captain DiMarco. Then I will bring your luggage to your cabin."

"Oh, thank you so much."

~

LORENZO WAITED on the bridge for word that Francesca had boarded. He was busy going over charts and preparing for the voyage across the Pacific. Notifications came in from all parts of the ship. The one he just received informed him that the *Diamond of the Seas* is fully fueled.

This was the second cruise of his ten weeks on. He'd spent the previous ten weeks island hopping in the Caribbean. He hadn't gone home to Palermo in ten years, not since he left. During his time off, he played guest on another Contessa Line cruise. He even spent a few days with his cousin Giorgio Lombardo and his newly wedded wife Madeline at their summer home on Maui.

He glanced at his solid-gold wristwatch, waiting for Mario to call, letting him know Francesca had come up the gangway. He'd told his steward to escort her to the VIP lounge where Lorenzo would meet them. Thirty minutes later, Mario called, telling him they were on board, and Francesca was waiting for him.

Lorenzo stepped off of the elevator. Standing with his steward was a beautiful woman. His breath caught. *Is this her? No, it couldn't be. She is petite and curvy, a woman now. Where are the pigtails and the smudges of dirt on her face?* Her beauty left him speechless, as his eyes roamed her body from head to toe. She wore a wide-brim raffia hat and black cat-eye sunglasses. Pink lipstick on sexy, pouty lips and her blond, flowing hair reached to just above her tiny waist. A black spaghetti-strap blouse was tucked into the small waistband of her leopard-print shorts. Her legs were tanned and toned. Pink-polished toenails peeked out of her espadrilles, the straps tied around her dainty ankles. She held a designer bag over one shoulder.

An urge to see a hell of a lot more of her settled over him and in the next instant, he wanted to cover her from prying eyes. *This is certainly an odd feeling. Because it's your friend's sister and she's just a kid.* He nodded to Mario, and the steward left. "Hello, Francesca. I would never have recognized you."

"I know, isn't it crazy? I'm all grown up." She grinned at him, posing with her hand on her hip and one knee pushed forward. "I'd recognize you anywhere, Lorenzo, or do I have to call you Captain DiMarco?"

"Lorenzo is good... or... Zo. Remember the nickname you gave me?"

She covered her mouth. "Tee-hee, I can't believe you remember that."

"No one but you would have dared to call me Zo." He looked at her. "I don't think I can call you Imp anymore... Are you tired from the flight?"

"Oh no, I'm too excited to be tired. This is my first trip to the US. I want to walk around, maybe grab an American hamburger and a drink. Will you show me around the boat?"

"Ship. It's a ship." He nudged her shoulder with his.

She smiled up at him. "Of course, I will remember that. Now, how about that hamburger?"

"Sure, a buffet lunch and BBQ is being served on the Lido Deck. I can keep you company for a bit. Then I'll have to be on the bridge for a few hours before we set sail."

"Can I see the bridge and you at work?" she asked with a voice full of excitement.

"Maybe tomorrow, while we're at sea, you can come up to the bridge. Now, let's go get you that burger."

He led her to a private elevator and pressed the button for

the Lido Deck. As the elevator doors slid open, the calypso music from the live band pounded around them.

"Oh, this is great." Francesca danced off the elevator to the beat of the music.

Waiters dressed in festive outfits carried trays of different types of cocktails. Several passengers sat on deck chairs around the pool, while others sat at tables, eating. Many wheeled their suitcases around. The all clear sounded, and the passengers were invited to proceed to their cabins. Some left, while others stayed, enjoying the music and their lunch.

Lorenzo grinned as he followed Francesca. He lightly put his hand on the small of her back and said, "This way." Leading her to a roped-off area with several tables and chairs in the shade. A waiter approached holding a round tray in the palm of one hand above his shoulder, dancing the two step. He stopped short, the smile on his face vanishing.

"It's okay, my guest is old enough to drink."

"Yes, sir, Captain DiMarco. I'm sorry I didn't expect to see you on deck."

"What kind of fruity drinks are these?" Francesca asked in flawless English, peering at the tray.

The waiter said, "One of our specialties, miss. Piña colada."

"Yummy, but I'll need some food in me first."

Lorenzo stepped closer to Francesca; her sweet scent teased his nostrils, reminding him of home.

"Captain, allow me to bring you both some food," the waiter said.

"Can you bring me one of those famous American hamburgers with the works?" Her excitement spilled into her voice.

Lorenzo read the tag on the waiter's uniform. "Sam, nothing for me but bring some fries with the burger and a bottle of mineral water." Lorenzo slid a chair from the table for Francesca to sit.

"Yes, sir. Right away, sir." He placed the cocktail and a napkin on the table where she sat, and then he hurried away.

Lorenzo took the chair next to her.

"He was surprised to see you, Zo."

The sky paled in comparison to her blue gaze. He forgot how vibrant the color of her eyes were, or maybe he never paid attention to the Imp. "Yes, I rarely come up here and especially not on turnaround day. I'm too busy overseeing the ship, preparing for departure. We docked at four this morning and will sail at four this afternoon. Twelve hours to unload and load up."

"Wow, that's amazing… Thank you for meeting me." Her hand touched his forearm.

Francesca Russo's warm touch, her blue eyes, and the smile on her pink-stained lips sent a jolt of pleasure through him. *She's a kid and just trying to be nice.*

"I guess you heard what happened to my friend Stella and why I'm traveling alone."

"Yes, too bad she broke her leg, and the doctors didn't want her flying."

"My parents weren't happy with me being alone. Then Gus said he would call you… That's all right, isn't it? I don't need anyone to watch out for me, so you're off the hook, Zo."

"I'm here if you need me. When we get to Maui, Giorgio and Maddie will be there with Ricardo and my sister-in-law, Liz. We can visit with them."

"That will be fun. I heard Giorgio got married. I haven't seen him in about the same amount of time as you. Ten years!" She laughed. "Remember how I would follow Gus, Gio, and you around? My brother hated it, trying to bribe me with money to go away."

"I remember you were a brat. Always in trouble."

"Oh, but you were the one who made me feel better, buying me a gelato… Vanilla, my favorite."

The waiter arrived with her food and placed the plate on the table in front of her. She slipped her cell phone out of her purse and took a selfie of her eating her first American hamburger. She leaned into Lorenzo and snapped another picture. "I'm going to send it to Gus." She turned the screen toward him. "Look how cute we are."

He smiled.

"Do you mind if I post it to my Instagram?"

"Post away, Imp."

While they talked, she finished the entire burger and the fries, as well as the piña colada and the bottle of water. Then she sat back and patted her stomach. "Maybe later I can find a gelato, but right now, I think I will go to my cabin and unpack."

"Good idea." He glanced at his Rolex. "I can walk you to your cabin before I have to be on the bridge. The first night is usually casual as the guests settle in. We will have a mandatory muster drill that you will have to take part in. Then you should probably have dinner in the dining room, so you can meet your tablemates. Later in the evening, one of the nightclubs will have a meet and greet for all the passengers and another for the single guests."

"That sounds like fun."

"Yes. You should walk around and acquaint yourself with the ship. I'm sure there's a pocket map in your cabin."

They rode the elevator to Deck 3, and he walked her down the narrow hall to her cabin. At the door, she turned to him. "I know I'm at the bottom of the ship. I don't even have a porthole, but I paid for the entire trip with my own money." She put her arms around his neck and rose on her toes to kiss first one cheek, then the other. "Thank you, Lorenzo."

CHAPTER 2

*F*rancesca watched Lorenzo as he left. Oh, so tall with lean, narrow hips, his white uniform pants accenting his butt as he sauntered away from her. *OMG, he's more handsome than I remember. He smells good too, just like the sea, with an undertone of exotic spices. And when he speaks English, he has a delicious Italian accent, subtle but there in his deep, sexy voice.*

Francesca wanted to be settled before they set sail, so she hurried to unpack. Her cabin was small, with twin beds separated by a tiny nightstand. A chair in one corner with a wardrobe. She opened the door to the ensuite. Shower, commode and sink. *It's a good thing I'm not claustrophobic.* She found her restaurant assignment and table seating, along with the map Lorenzo mentioned on the night stand. She opened the wardrobe to find several life jackets. Lorenzo had said he didn't tolerate any tardiness or not following directions from the crew. The drill wasn't for fun and games. She thought that was funny because she remembered he was always for fun and games.

In Palermo, women were always chasing him, her

brother, and Giorgio. There was never a shortage of women whenever they were around. She'd heard some crazy rumors about Lorenzo and from what she recalled, he'd left a trail of broken hearts from Palermo to Venice and beyond the borders of Italy. The most she'd ever gotten was him ruffling her hair and calling her *Imp*. Well, she was a kid back then… but now. Oh, man…wow.

Seeing him today in his white uniform shirt, the edge of his short sleeves fit snug around his biceps, and when she touched his forearm, she had to control herself and not caress his arm. He wasn't very hairy, but there was enough black, silky hair covering the muscles in his arms to be sexy, and her reaction surprised her. She wanted to see more of his body. *What did he look like naked? I'll bet he's covered in muscles.* She closed her eyes for a moment, trying to envision him. Michelangelo's *David* came to mind.

Lorenzo went back to the bridge. He entered the code to unlock the steel door and walked in. His officers were busy with preparations. It was two hours before they would set sail. The blue water of San Diego Bay was dotted with sailboats. They were the only cruise ship in port today. This was an oddity because San Diego was a busy port.

He brewed himself an espresso, then he and his second in command went down the list of procedures. He was in contact with the harbor pilot. At three-thirty, he received the green light that all the passengers were on board. Lorenzo picked up the phone to the engine room.

"Get the generators ready, maneuvering mode." He did another quick check before he flipped the switch on the ship-wide communication and made an announcement. "Good afternoon, ladies and gentlemen. This is Captain

DiMarco. On behalf of myself and the entire crew, welcome aboard the *Diamond of the Seas*. I've been informed that all of the passengers are on board, and we will depart in ten minutes. That's one zero minutes."

At exactly four p.m., he gave the order to sound the horn. Lorenzo didn't think of his two ladies. He thought about the next sixteen days with Francesca Russo. He shook his head and took command of his vessel. "All port thrusters." They inched away from the dock. "Easy, that's it." His ship cleared the dock and moved out. "All aft thrusters. Steady due west." He leaned his hip against the arm of his leather captain's chair and gave the order to sound the alarm for the muster drill.

He liked the precision of his officers and staff. Once the drill was over, and he went over the report, he turned the bridge command over to his second in command. It had been a long day. Turnaround day always was. He'd been up since two this morning, so he walked the few steps from the bridge to his cabin, ready to make his log entries, have some dinner, and go to sleep. Mario had turned down his bed and brought him a panino and a glass of wine.

He paid his steward's salary with his own money. His officers knew he had his own billions of dollars but didn't accept any special treatment from his brother, the CEO of DiMarco Enterprises, or his cousin Giorgio Lombardo, the chairman of the board.

His last thoughts before he drifted to sleep were of Francesca. No longer a little girl, but a grown woman. Did she have a boyfriend at home?

Francesca teetered between apprehension and excitement. After the muster drill. She went back to her cabin on deck 3 to shower and change into a casual outfit for dinner. Choosing one of the many summer dresses she'd designed and made especially for this vacation. Tying her hair up in a messy bun, she applied eyeliner and then mascara to her long lashes. Francesca put her key card, a tube of lip gloss and the folding map of the ship into her gold cross body purse. She checked herself in the mirror one last time, happy with her choice of low heel gold sandals before she left to find the main dining room.

She walked down the narrow orange and yellow carpeted hallway noticing that some of the cabin doors were decorated with banners that said, Happy Birthday or Bon Voyage and one must have been put up in a hurry, as the pineapple was upside down. She giggled as she walked to the front of the ship, reminding herself it was called forward. She found the bank of eight elevators that would take her to the restaurant deck.

As her elevator stopped at each of the next five decks, it became crowded with passengers also going to the main dining room. Once off the elevator on this deck, the color scheme changed to blues and greys. The design in the carpet were swirls of deep blue to pale blue. There was a hum of excitement from the other passengers waiting in line to walk through the main entrance of the dining room. Francesca took her place in the queue as the line moved fairly quickly.

The maître d' dressed in a black suit and white dress shirt with a dark tie. On his right breast pocket, his badge with his name, position, and country he was from. A line of waiters stood behind him to the right and left. He looked at each guest's room key and then had a waiter escort them to their table. When it was Francesca's turn, she was prepared showing her room key to the maître d' with her table assignment. "Welcome Miss Russo, please follow this server. He will escort you to your table."

"Hello Miss, your table is here on the main floor." She glanced around and saw that the restaurant was three levels high and the main floor was open to all. They walked around to one side. Square tables for four and larger rectangular tables for six to twelve passengers lined the wall by the overly large rectangular windows. Sheer curtains covered the windows. It was dusk, but you could still see the magnificent view of the ocean. She would never grow tired of that.

Her waiter stopped at a round table covered in the palest blue tablecloth. A napkin of the same color sat on the center of each plate. Eight high back leather chairs circled the table. He pulled out the last empty seat for Francesca. "Hello all," she said, as the waiter pushed her chair in for her.

The woman to her right said, "Hello, my name is Claire O'Malley. We've already introduced ourselves."

"I'm Francesca Russo and you can call me Frankie." Then one by one the other women began introducing themselves to her.

Their server came over. "Good evening, ladies. I will have the pleasure of serving you along with my two assistants." He handed them each a leather bound menu. They stopped chatting long enough to order appetizers, salad and main course.

Then Claire said, "There is so much to do on board. I want to try the zip line. What about you Frankie?"

"I want to try that too and surfing."

"We should plan to do that together," Claire said and looked around the table. "Anyone else interested?"

Another said, "I signed up for surfing lessons when we get to our first port."

"I chose Volcanoes National Park," Francesca said.

"Me too."

"I did too."

"Maybe we can all go together," Claire said.

The dessert menu was placed in front of her and Francesca realized she was relaxed and calmer about traveling alone.

Once dinner and dessert were over, some of her table mates excused themselves. Claire asked, "Do you want to walk around the deck? The nightclub won't open for another hour. Then they have a singles mixer in the night club under the stars. The ceiling becomes opaque."

"Okay, that sounds like fun. This is my first cruise, and this is such a big ship. I don't think I'll ever find my way around."

Claire laughed at that. "I've been cruising for years. By the time the cruise ends you'll figure it out."

"I hope so." They walked out onto the promenade deck. The night was warm and the slight breeze was comfortable. Some passengers were sitting at tables sipping cocktails while others sat on chaise lounges enjoying the night sky.

Claire said, "I'm booked on the Mexico cruise after this."

"Really?"

"Yes, I plan on seeing the world one cruise at a time. Since my divorce two years ago, I do something like this booking back to back cruises. I'm not bragging, but I will still have time to use around the holidays too."

"That's fantastic."

One of their tablemates hurried over. "Hi, are you two going to the singles mixer?"

"Yes we are," said Francesca.

"I hope to meet someone at the mixer tonight. You know, just a companion for the cruise," Josie said. Her short mop of brown curls bouncing as she spoke.

"That should be fun. Plus, there is so much to do on board." They walked into the nightclub happy to meet other singles.

Francesca had a good time dancing and was looking forward to her first vacation alone.

The following day, Lorenzo was busy on the bridge, but

not so much that he didn't think of Francesca. Mid-morning, he asked his steward Mario to find Francesca and give her the note that he'd written. "Mario, wait for a reply," he said.

"Yes Captain."

Mario found her on the pool deck, lying in the sun. "Hello, miss, this is from Captain DiMarco." He handed her the embossed envelope. She took out the note card, and Mario watched as a smile spread across her lips. Nodding, she said, "Yes, tell him I would love a tour of the bridge. I'll be there."

"Yes, miss. I will let the captain know."

Lorenzo waited on the Lido deck and at three sharp, she met him.

Francesca looked cheery and excited in a pink mini dress and cream espadrilles. "Thank you, Lorenzo. I thought you forgot."

How could I? She's all I thought about. I even dreamt of her riding me. Her breasts made his mouth water. "Did you meet anyone at the meet and greet?"

She pushed her long blond hair off her face. "Yes, a few of my tablemates and I went. We met a group of singles from the early seating, and we spent the night dancing. It's really lots of fun."

"That's good. Tonight, at the captain's cocktail party, I will introduce you to the cruise director. He's from London, and I know he has lots of specialty dancing scheduled. Everything from line dances to waltzing."

"Oh yes, I know. He stopped by the nightclub last night and introduced himself. He told us about some of the dancing classes and other activities, like the zipline and rock climbing. There's a surfing pool. I want to learn how to surf, and there are three adult pools—" She giggled. "Why am I telling you? I'm sure you know better than me."

"Yes, there is really so much to do on board. Surfing is

fun. You'll love that." He punched in a code on the keypad beside the metal door to the bridge.

"Wow, the bridge is kept locked?"

"Yes, always. It's for security. This way," he said as he lead her into the space. Francesca's eyes rounded when she saw two security guards on either side of the door.

Another officer said, "Captain on the bridge."

"At ease, men," Lorenzo said as he walked further into the large rectangular room that spanned the ship with wings extending out over the water on each side.

He walked her around the bridge, introducing her to his officers and pointing out the various stations with their electronic instruments. She looked around the bridge. "Where is the steering wheel?"

He bent to whisper, "Like the big wooden one with spokes?"

"Yes, like that."

"There is none. This is how we steer the ship." Lorenzo pointed to a small wheel.

"That looks more like one on an airplane... maybe smaller." She pouted. "I'm disappointed."

"No need, Imp. You can still turn the wheel."

"Really! You'll let me drive the ship?" She bounced on her toes.

"No." He shook his head. "We're on autopilot."

"Oh." She sounded disappointed again. "The whole way to our first port?"

"Yes and no. We monitor the route constantly and make corrections manually for wind and speed."

"That's really interesting. I'm amazed. Thank you for showing me around. This is so much more than I thought."

"Where are you off to now?"

"I'm going on deck and sit in the shade, maybe grab a gelato and just enjoy the ocean breeze and the sun."

"I'll walk with you if you like."

She bumped her hip into him, saying, "I thought you'd never ask."

They took his private elevator a few decks down. He led her to the gelato bar. There was both indoor and outdoor seating. "Go find a table, Imp. I'll get the gelato."

"Okay, outside under one of the umbrellas. Is that good?"

"Yes." The ship glided smoothly on autopilot, and Lorenzo brought her a waffle cone filled with vanilla gelato. They sat at a white round table under a blue-and-white-striped umbrella.

Francesca licked her gelato. "Mmmm, yummy." She took the top rounded scoop of gelato into her mouth, and his dick came alive. *Does she know what she's doing? Smacking those sexy lips together and closing her eyes in pure pleasure. This must be how she looks when she comes. Get a grip, man.* He had to stop thinking of her like that. After all, she was his friend's baby sister. But to look at her now, she was a grown woman capable of bringing him to his knees. *How would her mouth feel on my dick?*

"The bridge was amazing. All the people that work up there and the view. Oh my."

"The best in the house." His gaze roamed over her face and down to her fabulous breasts. Some of the passengers strolling by recognized him and waved. Lorenzo nodded.

"You must see dolphins and other marine life?"

"Yes, and sometimes a whale or two. The watch lets me know, so I can make an announcement to the passengers so they can enjoy it too."

A young woman crew member Lorenzo recognized as part of the waitstaff approached. She smiled. "Hello, Captain DiMarco." Then she turned to Francesca. "Miss, thank you for fixing that loose button on my uniform blouse."

"It was my pleasure. I'm glad I could help you."

"Captain, she's a lifesaver. Well, if you will pardon me, I'll get back to work."

The young woman walked away, and Lorenzo said, "You carry needle and thread?"

"Yes. Stella, my friend, the one who broke her leg, and I went to fashion school. We spent two semesters in Milan and one in Florence, so yes. I always have a sewing kit on me."

He shook his head. "Very interesting." *What else do you have on you?* He wanted to strip her and make her beg him to throw her over his desk and take her until she begged him to satisfy her sweet pussy. He liked clean-shaven pussy if he had to go down on a woman, but he preferred they take him into their mouths.

"Zo, are you listening?"

He sat up straight, his jaw clenched, before he said, "Of course I'm listening. What else would I be doing?"

They sat and talked about home, how Gus and Sara enjoy living in Erice. Their kids and the restaurant they own.

"You talked about school and career, but…" Lorenzo held her eyes. "Is there anyone special in your life?"

"No. I'm focusing on my career." She took a last lick of the gelato. "I've taken a lot of your time and now, I realize how busy you are, so I'm going back to my cabin. Will I see you later?"

I hope so. "Yes, tonight is the captain's cocktail party." He stood, subtly adjusting himself.

Francesca rose, slinging her purse over her shoulder, and said, "That's right. I have my invitation in my cabin. I can get there by myself. Thank you for the tour and the gelato." She kissed him on both cheeks and then turned to go. The mini dress clung to the curve of her hips and caressed her butt.

What was wrong with him? His dick insisted on making him aware of her and the way she licked that gelato. He should have ordered her a cup, but then what would she do with that spoon? He could just imagine the way she would lick the spoon. He left for the bridge, determined to block her out of his mind. *She's Gus' baby sister, she's Gus' baby sister.* He chanted. *Stop these thoughts. Wait until you get to Hilo and your two women.*

CHAPTER 3

The captain's cocktail party was held mid-ship in the grand salon, which spanned the main deck. The atrium-style floor plan was open and banks of glass elevators surrounded the area. Five decks above starlight glinted through the glass dome. Lorenzo and his officers were dressed in their navy-blue formal evening wear. The waiters carried trays of cocktails, while others brought appetizers around. An orchestra played music near the dance floor.

Lorenzo stood with his senior officers in the receiving line, greeting the guests. He knew that his officers bet on how many room keys he would collect. Some of the women were discreet, shaking his hand with their plastic key card in their hand. "Oh, Captain, perhaps we can share a drink." Others were much more obvious, including pressing their breasts against him while whispering, "Captain, I would love for you to *come* to my cabin."

Once the receiving line ended, he would give all the keys to his steward. Mario would order flowers from the ship's florist. The florist called it, *The Captain's Special.* Lorenzo made sure that each of the lovely women would receive a delivery of one dozen red roses. A note accompanied the bouquets expressing his regret that he couldn't enjoy their company.

The married ones or ones traveling with a significant other received a bottle of champagne and a very discreet note of regret. Lorenzo paid for all of this with his own money, not stiffing the cruise line. Even though his family owned the line, and he owned stock in DiMarco Enterprises.

Women were always throwing themselves at him, wanting photos, and some wanted to dance with the captain. The photos were allowed, but he didn't dance with the guests. Ever. He had women in every port without any reason to complicate his position. He set the standard. His crew couldn't fraternize with the passengers either. Once they debarked at their final port and no longer passengers on a Contessa Line cruise, then it wasn't his concern. But while on board, it was all business, making sure the passengers had a great experience without sex from the crew. He wouldn't tolerate any complications with the passengers or crew. He instilled severe penalties for breaking the rules. Several times that included immediate dismissal.

None of the crew were ever allowed to dance with the guests. In the dining room, though, it was different. The waiters would form conga lines and invite the guests to join.

Lorenzo liked the variety of women and would never settle for one the way his brothers had. Ricardo had Liz and a son. Gianni had Sofia; they'd met in kindergarten and hadn't been apart from that moment on. They married last New Year's Eve. He'd missed their wedding because he wouldn't return to Palermo.

The shocker was that his free and wild cousin Giorgio Lombardo got married on Valentine's Day to Madeline Watson, a bank executive. One minute he and Giorgio were partying in New York City before Christmas. His cousin abandons him to some beautiful women which Lorenzo took full advantage of. Giorgio flew him back to San Diego on his private jet and the next thing he learns that his cousin got married in Las Vegas!

He didn't want vanilla sex when he could have all the other flavors. He was the DiMarco family's black sheep and his aunt Angela, was the family's loose cannon. Even she had found someone and settled down. She was having twins. Now that was crazy.

He spoke with the guests, shaking hands, making small chit chat, and keeping an eye on the receiving line. It stretched on and on. Lorenzo could see the dance floor and the small cocktail tables. He looked for Francesca. Since this afternoon, when her pink tongue licked the gelato, every time he glanced toward her his dick sent him a message he was desperate to ignore. She was a beauty, and it was difficult for him to remember why he had imposed the no fraternizing with crew or guests rule.

He wanted to fraternize with Francesca all over the ship and in every position he could imagine. He was the captain, and the rules didn't apply to him if he chose not to follow them. Right now, he wanted her on her knees, taking his hard dick deep into her sexy mouth. *What would she look like with red lipstick on her puffy lips as she sucked his dick?* He had to stop, or this hard-on would never calm. He discreetly adjusted himself. For the hundredth time he remembered Gus—who trusted him—with his baby sister. He wouldn't let her temp him against his will.

She was here. Her throaty, sexy voice whispered, "Hello Captain DiMarco." She wore a satin floral print top in shades of blue with its off the shoulder large portrait collar and a deep v that drew the eye to her very desirable high breasts.

The pants were wide leg, flowing chiffon, of a solid lapis color and all he wanted was to strip her of her clothes.

"Hello, Ms. Russo, are you enjoying your vacation?" Her sultry scent drifted up and he took a breath, wanting more.

"Completely. Will you dance with me?"

"My apologies. I don't dance with the guests."

Oh, I'm sorry I didn't realize." Her look of disappointment wretched at his heart.

Until Ms. Russo came aboard he never had a problem following the rules he set. Each time she danced by his gaze followed. He hated that he'd told her no, he wouldn't dance with her. He didn't dance at these events. She was in that provocative, sexy outfit, laughing and dancing with the guests at the party. He wanted to dance with her spin her around the way that man was, hold her in his arms.

Earlier, Francesca introduced him to a passenger just the right age for her. He looked to be twenty-five but every time she laughed that seductive laugh of hers, all Lorenzo wanted to do was rip them apart.

Francesca's husky laugh made him want to take her in his arms and dance the night away. She was driving him crazy.

Lorenzo reminded himself that all he had to do was look at a woman, and she'd be his. God forbid if he winked or smiled at her. He had women in every port without any reason to complicate his position. No need to lust after his friend's sister. Ten years ago, when he turned his back on his father and Sicily, he made a conscious decision. No commitments, no family or marriage, just uncomplicated sex.

This cruise was longer than the usual Sunday to Sunday. She'd said that she chose the sixteen-day cruise to Hawaii for something different. He smirked to himself. *Since she came aboard, it's certainly been different.*

Relief flooded him, as the buzz of the receiving line was

finally subsiding. A few more hands to shake and then time for him to give a brief speech, and he could leave.

Again, he watched her dance by, and he had to force himself to concentrate on the guest whose hand he shook. *You don't need to babysit her. She's a grown woman, able to make her own decisions, so what's your problem? When she's near you, you want all the things you never wanted before... all the things you've denied yourself. You want vanilla sex!*

There was an unwritten law. *Don't mess around with your friend's sister. Keep that uppermost in your mind.* But when she casually brushed her hand on his arm, he... wanted more. He wanted to take her to bed and—what? Make love to her, only her... forever.

Lorenzo walked back to his cabin disgusted with himself, willing his hard-on away. He changed out of his formal uniform and went to the bridge to check on the night watch. He had a pile of work on his desk, so he went back to his cabin to sift through that. He couldn't concentrate on any of it. He found himself in the officer's elevator. The doors silently opened on the nightclub deck, and he wasn't sure why he did this. Who was he kidding? He was looking for her, the blond beauty who took his breath away.

He spotted her instantly. Francesca had changed into a hot pink mini dress that clung to every curve of her body. She was dancing, swaying her hips as her blond hair floated around her shoulders. She stood on towering silver stilettos. The hem of the pink dress was high up on her thighs. She lifted her arms over her head, continuing to swing her hips.

Lorenzo held his breath, waiting to see the color of her panties. The man she was dancing with pulled her into him, and she threw her head back as she shimmied against him. Then he spun her out of his embrace before pulling her back into him, swaying with her to the final beats of the music. One of his hands brushed over a buttock. Lorenzo took a step forward, wanting to rip them apart before he stopped himself.

Francesca leaned against her dance partner, laughing. His arm was tight around her waist as he led her back to their table.

Lorenzo's jaw clenched, as he glanced at the other couples before he left and walked along the deck, breathing in the sea air. Why should he be angry at the way she danced? It was her business if she didn't object to the way her partner danced with her.

The guests were here to have fun. She was a guest… okay, his friend's sister, but a guest nonetheless. He liked commanding this vessel, and that was all. On land, he could have all the sex he wanted, and he did. Women fell at his feet to please him. He could wait until Hilo. He wasn't a teenager in lust. He was a grown man in charge of his libido. A jumble of emotions ran its course before he buried them all.

He walked past an alcove along the deck and found his chief engineer gazing out into the blackness.

Lorenzo spoke in Italian, "Enjoying the night?"

"*Buona sera,* Captain. Tonight, I like the calm of the ocean."

"Yes. It's welcome. How are you?"

"Just taking a break. My wife and I video chatted earlier, and she wants a divorce. She said she didn't sign on for me being gone so many months at a time." He sighed. "I know she's right, so I told her I wouldn't fight her. The sea is my life."

Lorenzo patted his chief engineer and friend on the back. "Come by my cabin if you want to, we can have a drink and talk."

"*Grazie mille,* Captain."

Lorenzo waited for the officer's elevator and went back to his cabin. His jaw clenched and unclenched before he muttered, "Women." He poured himself a whiskey and sat at his desk, going over paperwork and his emails, both business and personal.

There was an email from his brother Ricardo, the CEO of DiMarco Enterprises, reminding him that he would be in Maui and wanted to firm up his new position as COO of the Contessa Line. He cursed under his breath and deleted the email. He would not be forced into that position. He could never forgive his father for his high-handed attempt to force him––so he stayed away.

He sighed and slid the balcony door open. Breathing the briny ocean air he walked out and paced the length of his balcony. The music from the nightclub drifted down to him, and he thought of Francesca dancing. He brought his whiskey glass to his lips, tipped his head back, and drank the whole of it in one shot. He grit his teeth. The warmth in his stomach from the drink didn't help. He turned and went back inside. He lay in his bed for hours, tossing and turning until he finally fell asleep.

His alarm woke him the next morning. He groaned at the painful hard-on he had. The cold shower almost worked. Then he shaved and dressed for the day. He kept busy on the bridge, trying not to think of Francesca. At midday, he went to one of the conference rooms below deck where the new crew members who had come aboard in San Diego waited for him. The men and women sat around the table, each with a note pad, pen, and bottle of water in front of them. He didn't know if this was their first time working on a cruise ship or if they'd signed previous contracts. He also didn't care what jobs they held on board; that was for their supervisors.

He stood facing the group. "On this ship, your safety role is the most important position you have. If the ship goes into a state of emergency, you need to know your emergency station and what is expected of you. Make sure you know the number for the bridge. You must know where additional life vests are kept."

He looked at each new hire before he said, "What do you do if a child is lost? What do you do if a parent says they're missing their child? Crew drills are performed often and at all different times. I cannot stress enough the importance of these drills. This will prepare you *not* to panic, because, if you panic, and the passengers panic, then we're screwed. Remember this. Contract or not, if you foul up in your safety duties, I will not hesitate to terminate you on the spot. Understand?"

He heard the chorus of, "Yes, Captain DiMarco."

"Dismissed."

He made his rounds along with his chief safety officer and then went back to the bridge.

Tonight was movie night on the big screen under the stars. He found Francesca on the lido deck. She reclined on a deck chair in one of those provocative outfits she seemed to favor; this one was a cut out and just about covered the areolas of her breasts. Her cleavage and the fleshy underside of her breasts were bare. Thin chords of fabric wrapped around her torso to her hips where the fabric clung to her. *What the hell is she wearing?* She sat next to the same young couple from the nightclub. She sipped a drink from a straw, the little yellow paper umbrella off to one side.

His brow lifted; he couldn't be mistaken—the couple chatting with Francesca sat on deck chairs with pineapple-shaped towel fasteners. When clipped in that manner, the pineapples were upside down. He knew the code for swingers, but did Francesca? Now, for the third time when she was around, an unfamiliar emotion gripped him. Definitely lust but more than that. Protection. He had the urge to take her away and hide her. Deep in the recesses of his mind, the strange compulsion not to share her with anyone ever overtook his thoughts.

Francesca, a big smile on her beautiful face and her blond hair cascading over bare shoulders, waved to him. Now he had no choice but to go over and greet them. He recognized the woman as one of the many who had slipped her room key into his hand at the cocktail party.

"Hello, are you enjoying the cruise thus far?"

"Yes, Captain. I certainly am." She leaned forward in a provocative manner. "Your cocktail party was a delight."

The man with her stroked her arm before he said, "We especially *love* the at-sea days. Resting during the day and clubbing at night."

"That's wonderful. I'm happy to hear that you are doing what you like." Then he turned to Francesca. "Francesca, have you eaten dinner?"

"No. Not yet, Captain DiMarco."

"If you want, we can have a late supper together."

"Yes. I would like that." She stood and said to the couple, "You'll have to excuse me. Captain DiMarco is a friend of my brother. Maybe we can meet later at the nightclub or tomorrow at the pool."

"Good night, Frankie, Captain," the woman said.

Once he and Francesca were out of earshot, he snapped, "When did you meet that couple?"

Francesca gasped at his tone. She stretched her neck to look up at him. "Yesterday at your cocktail party and earlier today, we met in the passageway. They're a few cabins away from me, and I told them I liked their door decoration."

"What was it?" he asked, tipping his head to one side.

"A pineapple, but it was purposefully upside down." She giggled. "I thought that someone was making a joke. Then they asked me to join them for the movie tonight."

He grunted. "That was all. No mention of what it may

signify?" He snapped his long, tanned fingers. "And then poof, they—just like that—invite you to the movie?"

Why does he seem upset? She frowned. "Last night, I went to the nightclub, and I saw them with Joe, the person I was dancing with at your cocktail party. He's a travel companion of theirs. He's going to meet us at the club later tonight."

"I see," he said.

His frown surprised her. *What's got him upset?* "Is everything alright?"

"Yes, of course. What would you like for dinner? We can go to one of the specialty restaurants… or if you prefer, I can have the chef prepare dinner in my cabin."

She smoothed a hand over her hip. "I'm really not dressed to sit in a fancy restaurant. What can the chef prepare?" Heat spread across her body as his gaze traveled the length of her. His obsidian eyes made her weak in the knees. The black-as-night gaze stopped at her breasts. Sparks flew as she fought the urge to cover herself, rethinking her choice of dress. Her nipples tightened. His gaze moved lower, and a new sensation, stronger than ever before, pulsed between her legs. He looked into her eyes. Her heart skipped a beat, and her knees wobbled.

"For me, anything I want." His husky whisper sizzled up her spine.

OMG, what are we talking about? Oh yes, food. Her breath rushed out of her. "You choose. I can go change—"

"No, you're on vacation. Be comfortable." He smiled at her. "It's a pretty dress. We can have supper in my dining room near the bridge." He led her to a nook with one elevator door. He punched in a code, and the doors silently opened. "This way, Francesca." He put his hand at the small of her back. Did she imagine his thumb brushing over her sensitized skin, sending pulses of desire into her core?

"Is this your private elevator?" Her pulse raced, and she thought she sounded breathless.

"Yes, one of them. There's another mid-ship and one more aft." He sounded so official.

Once the elevator stopped, and they got off, he walked a few steps and stopped in front of a door on which the placard read, Captain Lorenzo DiMarco.

"After you, Francesca."

She gasped. "This is your cabin? It's a luxury apartment." She stepped onto a multi colored Persian rug and glanced around the living room. Two caramel colored leather sofas faced each other with two wing chairs at either side. A coffee table separated the two sofas and a large flatscreen television hung on one wall. In the dining room a crystal chandelier sparkled over a highly polished wood table surrounded by eight high-back upholstered seats. She joked, "I thought a room similar to mine, bed, bathroom, wardrobe. I don't even have a port hole. You have a terrace and…" She turned to look at him. "Is that your own pool?"

He unfastened the top three buttons of his white uniform shirt. "Some of the perks of being the captain."

She couldn't bring her eyes away from the black chest hair that peeked out from his shirt. Then Lorenzo stood with his feet braced apart and his hands clasped behind his back. The first time she saw him stand like that was yesterday on the bridge. She called it the Sea Captain's stance. His narrow waist and dare she look lower, at his thighs. They were like tree trunks outlined in his white uniform pants. He'd ordered dinner while they rode in the elevator. "Would you like an aperitivo?" Lorenzo sauntered over to the bar.

"Yes, do you have Prosecco?"

"Of course."

She followed him over to the mahogany topped bar.

Lorenzo took out two glasses and poured the drink into both. Taking the glass of bubbly wine, he'd poured for her.

"A toast to your first vacation alone."

"I was worried once Stella had to stay home. I've never been out of the EU. Well… not true. I went to Dubai with Gus and Sara. I helped take care of the kids. The baby is a handful, and they didn't want to leave him home, so I offered to help."

"I heard. He must take after you, Imp."

She smiled at him, then said, "I'm so glad that I continued with my plans. After Gus called you, I felt better. When I made the booking, I knew DiMarco Enterprises owned the Contessa Line, but I didn't know you were the captain of this ship."

"This is the third week of my ten weeks on."

"Then I'm lucky you're here. I didn't realize you worked like that. You haven't been back home?"

"No." *Go home for what? Listen to my father, hear the disappointment in his voice.*

The door buzzer sounded. "That must be our dinner." Lorenzo opened the door.

"Evening, Captain."

"Mario, you can set the food on the table."

"Yes, sir."

"You remember Miss Russo?"

"Yes, sir. Hello, miss."

"Hi, Francesca is good. You don't have to be so formal with me."

"Thank you, Miss Francesca," Mario said as he set the food on the sidebar.

Once the steward left, he and Francesca sat at the polished mahogany table to eat. "So, where was I?" he said. "Ah yes, do you have a boyfriend?" He bit into a shrimp from the plate of fritto misto, aware that he hadn't asked her that.

Francesca ran her pink nail-polished index finger along the rim of her wine glass. "No." She moved her head from side to side. "No boyfriend… they're messy. Right now, I want to focus on my fashion designs."

"Messy. That's a funny word. How so?"

She shrugged one bare shoulder and the band of yellow fabric pulled tight across her breasts defining the outline of her nipples. "They just are. Very demanding and interested in what they want with no regard to your wishes. Always trying to convince you they know best."

She gazed into his eyes, her blue eyes bright. "Dinner was fabulous. Thank you."

He understood better than most that this was a subject she didn't want to talk about. "Would you care for anything else?" *Me.*

"Oh, no. I'm stuffed."

"Then let's go out on the balcony. I did say that I don't dance with the guests, but now that we're alone—"

Her smile almost brought him to his knees. "Oh yes, I would love to dance with you, Zo."

The music from his cabin played over the speaker on the balcony. He took Francesca into the circle of his arms while she looped her silky arms around his neck. She swayed against him, as her fragrance floated in the air. She felt so soft in his arms.

"I can't believe the blackness of the sky over the ocean. You can practically reach up and pluck the stars out of the sky. It's so beautiful, Lorenzo."

"The sea is amazing at night," he said as they swayed to the music.

Francesca rested her head on his chest. "Do you have to go back to the bridge?" she asked in a low voice.

"No, the watch is capable. Will you go to the club

tonight?" He could stay like this forever, holding her petite curves in his arms.

"I was thinking about it. I had fun there last night. But you holding me and dancing with me now is much better."

"What about the couple you were going to see the movie with?" He knew he was probing and couldn't quite think why.

"They were nice. I mentioned that they were at the night-club too. Tomorrow, they're having a party in Joe's suite, and they invited me."

He stopped dancing and led her to the rail on the balcony. "Did they say what kind of party?"

She turned to look at him, her eyes wide. "You know, Zo, it's interesting you should say that. I had the feeling they were quizzing me to see if I was interested. They said their parties got pretty wild and if I didn't want to stay, I could leave."

His belly clenched, but he kept his voice smooth. "No pressure, that's good."

"I told them I'm not into drugs, because I'm not. Then Alice said we get high in other ways. So, I was confused."

He decided blunt was best. "Francesca, they're swingers."

Her brow furrowed, and her pink lips formed a straight line before she looked at him. "What? I don't understand. They like to party, what's wrong with that?"

I love it. "Nothing at all. It's just not a lifestyle that everyone enjoys."

"I'm not stupid or a child, but I'm getting the distinct feeling you're not telling me something, and I've missed it."

He wanted to drag her into his arms, but he kept his hands in his pockets. "Yes, Imp, you have... they like to switch partners."

Her mouth dropped open, and her brows shot up. "What? OMG, that's good for them but not for me. I've barely had—"

"Had what?"

In the dim light on the balcony, the cutest rosy blush covered her cheeks. "Nothing, never mind."

He held her gaze. *What was she going to say? What would she think if she knew I liked sex with two women, sometimes three or four at the same time.* He walked over to where she leaned against the railing. "Francesca, are you okay?"

She tipped her head to the side, and the gentle breeze ruffled her hair. "Mmm, yes, I'm perfectly all right." She glanced at him. "It's just that I didn't really think that was a thing."

He didn't dare touch her although he ached to comfort her, hold her in his arms. He gentled his voice. "For certain people, it's what they like. No commitments, just sex, with someone other than their spouse or significant other."

"Um... I guess but—ah, I... didn't know. I think I'll go back to my cabin now—I don't feel like going to the club."

"I'll walk you back." He wouldn't take no for an answer. She looked mortified; the color had drained from her heart-shaped face. *What else did they say to her?*

She smiled up at him. "Thanks, Zo. I'm glad you're here."

CHAPTER 4

The sea was calm. Lorenzo relaxed in his black leather captain's chair, admiring the blue waters. No white caps, just his ship slicing through the Pacific Ocean on its way to their first port. He chatted with his chief engineer. At midday, his cell phone rang. He was the only one allowed personal calls while on duty. He glanced at the screen, *Gus Russo*.

He accepted the call and spoke in their Sicilian dialect. Then he listened as his friend said, "Francesca says she's lonely in her cabin, but I think she may have gotten involved with something that is too much for her."

His body tensed as he sat taller in his chair. "Did she say what happened?" He turned to his second in command and held his phone up, nodding to him, letting him know he was leaving the bridge.

He listened to Gus as he strode to his cabin. "Not much, something about another couple, but she wouldn't say more. I know I'm only her brother, but she's my baby sister... I'm concerned. First for her to call from the ship—I know that's expensive, and she doesn't have much money. But more important, I don't like her being alone. Can't you bring her to your suite?"

He rubbed the back of his neck. "I'll have a security guard posted at her door."

"Don't be ridiculous, she would hate that. She said you have an extra bedroom in your cabin. I'll feel better knowing you're keeping an eye on her… I know it's a lot to ask, but she sounded concerned."

Lorenzo groaned inwardly. He wanted to do more than keep an eye on her. Keep his hands on her, like last night when they danced. He wanted to kiss her, make love to her, and have her take him into her mouth. Now her own brother wanted to send the hen right into the wolf's domain. "Where is she?" he snapped.

"In her cabin."

He paced the length of his living room. "I'll go check on Francesca and have a talk with her."

"Thanks."

Lorenzo could hear the relief in his friend's voice. "*Ciao* Gus, and don't worry." He ended the call. Lorenzo shook his head, thinking how he could get out of this. He compressed his lips. Already feeling excitement run through his body at the thought of having her so close to him.

Yesterday, he'd asked his chief security officer to discreetly check out the couple and Joe. They weren't causing any problems on board and as long as no laws were broken, it was their business how they chose to spend their vacation. He needed to go and talk to Francesca.

TEN MINUTES LATER, Lorenzo was at her cabin door. The halls were narrower down here, and the outside cabins just had a small porthole that didn't open. The next deck down was the infirmary and crew quarters, same with the next deck. Below that was what was known as the I-95 corridor, running the length and width of the ship. Then lower down, the engine room and the brig.

He tapped, and she opened her door before the second tap. She looked beautiful in a white eyelet frilly dress that ended mid-calf and espadrilles on her feet. Her blond hair pulled over one shoulder, the ends forming shiny curls. He stretched out his hand. "Here, I brought you a gelato. Can I come in?"

She stepped aside, smiling at him.

He was lost. *Is there a hint of tears in her eyes?* "Vanilla, your favorite."

Her pink tongue licked the cone where some of the gelato had dripped before licking all the way to the top of the cream. "What flavor do you like?" Francesca had no idea how sensuous she sounded.

He sighed. "I like three scoops, chocolate sandwiched between pistachio and cherry."

Her brow furrowed before she looked at him. "That's a lot of gelato."

His eyes narrowed. "Tell me what happened."

Sitting on her bed, she shrugged. "Nothing that I would believe, but Lorenzo, I'm uncomfortable staying here. I can take care of myself but..." She licked her gelato. "I'm here in this cabin alone, and although nothing happened... I just feel that I didn't understand what they wanted from me and then when I said that wasn't a thing I'd be interested in... everyone can seek pleasure however they want, but that wasn't for me, Joe snickered and made it sound as if I misunderstood. I felt as if he was gaslighting me."

"I can have security here at your door—"

"No! That would be worse. They'd know... Anyway, I was more upset with the way he made me believe that I misunderstood. Sex for the sake of sex isn't for me." She pouted. "Why can't I stay with you, Zo? You have a two-bedroom cabin and a private pool and balcony. I promise to stay out of your way. You won't even know I'm around. I promise. Please, please."

He felt trapped in this tiny cabin. He would worry about her by herself. He let out a long breath. "Come on, I'll have my steward pack your belongings." She jumped up and threw her arms around his neck. "Oh, thank you, thank you—"

He lifted his brow. "Do I have your gelato in my hair and on my collar?"

She backed away, her blue eyes two big saucers. "No." She tipped her head to one side. "Well… maybe just… a little. It's vanilla; no one will ever notice." She covered her mouth and giggled at him.

He grumbled on the way to her bathroom. *Half woman, half imp, can I control myself?* Taking a towel, he wet it, rinsed his hair, and cleaned the gelato from his uniform.

"Come on, brat. I have to get back to the bridge."

Francesca grabbed her Never Full and stuffed her bathing suit into it, along with her wide-brimmed straw sun hat and her cat-eye sunglasses. "I'll take these with me, and then you can have the rest of my stuff moved to your cabin." She reached up on her toes, resting her hands on his shoulders, and kissed both his cheeks. "Thank you, Zo." Her subtle jasmine scent drifted around him. The urge to hold her soft curves in his arms and take her sensuous lips almost won. Then he remembered she was his friend's kid sister, and he was the captain of this vessel. She looped her arm through his and leaned against him. They walked to the elevator.

"I'll text Mario to pack your things and bring them to the guest bedroom."

He led her up to his cabin. Opening the door, he walked through the living room to the opposite side of the cabin.

"Here's your room. Mario will deliver your suitcase shortly, and you can settle in." She dropped her bag onto the queen size bed.

"Come to the living room," he said, walking out of her bedroom.

He was at the bar. "There's a fridge with beverages, some fruits and vegetables, dips. You can make popcorn in the microwave, and there are chips in the cabinet. If there's anything else you want, ask Mario."

The top of her head reached his shoulder as she smiled at him. "I'll probably have dinner in the dining room with my friends tonight. See what they're planning on doing."

"Yes, that sounds good." He strode over to his desk and removed a key from the center draw. "Here, Imp, an extra key to my cabin." He dropped it into the palm of her hand.

"Interesting. It's not a key card but a brass key." She stuffed it into her dress pocket.

He'd never given a woman access to his private domain on the ship or off, and a feeling he couldn't quite describe as warmth mixed with lust radiated through his body.

Lorenzo reminded himself that Hilo was over four days away. He wanted to increase the speed and get the ship there sooner so he could meet with his two ladies. That would take the edge off his lust and keep his dick calmer. He inflicted his own torture on himself, but he could keep his libido under control. Now he would have to be more vigilant, seeing how Francesca reacted to alternative lifestyles. Too bad. He was too jaded to change.

CHAPTER 5

When he returned from the bridge, Francesca was still out. Having a guest in his cabin was interesting. He tried to follow his normal routine, going over paperwork, having a nightcap, and unwinding, but all he could do was think of Francesca. It was two in the morning when he heard her come in, and that's when Lorenzo relaxed enough to fall asleep.

In the morning he showered, shaved, and dressed in a short-sleeve white uniform. Francesca's jasmine scent lingered in the air as he walked into the living room. A smile lifted the corners of his mouth when he saw her out on the balcony. She sat in one of the bright-orange cushioned chairs by a low table. Her knees were raised, and the heels of her bare feet were on the edge of the seat. She held a sketchpad in her hand and, next to her, sat a box with colored pencils. He slid the floor to ceiling glass door open. Lorenzo listened to the satisfying sound of his ship as it cut through the Pacific on its way to their first port.

Francesca turned, and his breath caught. A gentle breeze blew through her blond hair. She wore the most intriguing top. Two slashes of pastel pink fabric crisscrossed her fabulous breasts. It was all that covered her torso. Shorts in a similar fabric hung low on her tiny waist. His dick came alive.

"Good morning, Zo." She placed the pad and pencil down on the table next to her.

"Good morning. What are you drawing?" he said, coming over to glance at the pad.

She stood. "Usually clothes, like what I'm wearing." She did a little spin as she modeled her outfit. The curve of her bottom sent a zap of fire into his dick. "I designed it." She lifted her sketchpad from the table and handed it to him. "Here, look. Today, I drew this view of the ocean with that other ship in the distance. It's beautiful."

He admired her shapely body. "Yes, it definitely is beautiful."

"I'm jealous. You get to see this all the time and breathe in the fresh sea air. Palermo may be a port city, but it can be stuffy at times." She stretched her arms out. "This is fabulous."

He grinned. "I love the open sea and the fresh salt air. Have you had breakfast yet?"

"No, when I looked out and saw this view, I grabbed my sketch pad and rushed out to draw. I guess I can go to the dining room and eat."

"Stay with me if you like. I usually have an espresso and a pastry before I go to the bridge."

"I would like that. Can I get a cornetto or two and a double espresso?"

He remembered what a sweet tooth she had. "I have a better idea. Let's order a *granita and brioche*."

Her eyes rounded. "Oh yes. Chocolate and almond for me with cream. I'd love that."

"Then I'll order two of those." He picked up the phone

and placed the order with Mario. When he ended the call, he turned to her. "Francesca, when I'm not here, you can order anything you want. I left instructions with Mario. He'll take your clothes to have laundered, whatever you need."

"Thank you, Lorenzo."

"Zo."

"Oh, yes… Zo." A smile touched her sexy pink lips.

After the breakfast of espresso and that delicious special granita treat Lorenzo had suggested he went to the bridge. Francesca liked staying with him. She hadn't realized how busy he was or that he was on call twenty-four hours a day. She avoided Joe and the other couple. Not because of how they chose to live, but just how they made her feel foolish and immature. They had befriended quite a group of passengers and were having fun. That was nice, but she chose to steer clear of them. Just a friendly hello if they passed each other, nothing more.

Today, her plan was the zipline. One of her tablemates, Claire, met her at the entrance. They were going to take photos of each other zipping sixteen decks above the ocean. The attendant helped her into her harness, and Claire snapped a bunch of photos. Francesca would post the photos to her Instagram. Stella wouldn't believe it if she didn't have proof so Francesca would be sure to message her.

After the zipline she and Claire went for a stroll on the Sun deck. They stopped at the bar to grab two sparkling waters and then went to sit on one of the many chaise lounges at the stern of the ship. Francesca loved the uninterrupted view of the ocean and watched the trail of white and turquoise waves in the ships wake.

"Frankie, look at this photo of me. I look terrified," she laughed.

"OMG, that was just before you started across."

"I can't believe I did it. The zipline was fun after all." Claire, glanced at her wristwatch. "Oh, I have to go now. I promised Joan I'd meet her on the lido deck. Maybe we can meet later at the shops?"

"Yes, that's great. I want to go to the formal wear dress shop. How about in an hour and a half?"

"Okay, that's plenty of time. I can even shower and change," Claire said before she hurried off.

The at-sea days were so pleasant strolling on the decks during the day while the nights were filled with dancing, and the shows on board were Broadway quality. Francesca was happy to spend time alone or with her tablemates. They didn't know she'd moved into the captain's extra bedroom in his cabin.

She entered the cabin just as Lorenzo emerged from his bedroom. He was dressed in his dark-blue uniform.

"Hello, Zo. Why are you dressed so formal? It's only mid-morning."

"Today, I'm officiating two weddings."

"Really? I didn't know that was a real thing. I thought that only happened in the movies." She walked over to him and adjusted his tie.

His eyes narrowed. "Is that so, Imp? What do you think… how do I look?"

"I think you look very handsome."

"Where are you coming from? Dressed in a Contessa Line tee shirt."

She smiled up at him. "The zipline. It was fun… by the third time." She shrugged a shoulder. "Once I got used to it. I'm grateful I didn't pee my pants."

Lorenzo burst out laughing. "Yes, I'm glad as well. I could just hear the announcement, 'Captain to the zipline. We have a flood.'"

She felt the heat rise into her cheeks. "Back to you. So, do you really marry couples?"

"As the highest authority at sea being the captain and master of the ship. Yes…" He grinned at her. "It helps that I received a justice of the peace license as well."

"Oh you, always teasing me. Don't let me hold you up. You know you really do look very handsome." She leaned in and sniffed. "You smell good too."

"Behave, Imp."

She giggled. "I'm changing and going to the gift shops."

While waiting for Claire, Francesca stopped in front of the dress shop window to admire the selection evening fashions on display.

"Hey, Frankie. I haven't seen you around. I'm going to the singles nightclub tonight with Alice and some others. Want to meet us?"

"Hi, Joe. Thanks, but I'm busy tonight and won't be able to meet you guys."

"Oh, too bad. It will be a blast. I'll see you around."

"Yes, okay. Bye Joe."

Francesca waited for Claire and then they both went into the shop. She and Claire bought a dress each and some cute earrings. Then she went back to the captain's cabin. She called Mario and ordered a Greek salad, a piece of flat bread, and sparkling water for a late lunch. She hurried into her bedroom to put on her bright-yellow polka dot bikini. She had designed it, and Stella had sewn it. Then she went out to the balcony. Mario brought her meal. Francesca put on her airpods, ate her lunch, and listened to music. Then she lay on the chaise lounge to tan herself.

She must have fallen asleep because a noise woke her. She

turned on the chaise lounge to see Lorenzo looking down at her. "Hi, I must have dosed."

"Another few minutes and you would have burned your delicate skin." His husky voice sent a shiver of delight through her body.

She handed him the bottle of sunblock and rolled onto her stomach. "Will you apply some to my back?" There was nothing but silence for several seconds. Francesca turned to look up at him. "Zo?"

His sensuous lips were set in a grim line and his black brows were drawn together. He held the bottle between his long, lean fingers and stood there looking at her.

"What's wrong? Never applied sunblock to a woman's back?" she teased.

He lifted a dark brow at her before amusement flickered in the depths of his onyx eyes. Lorenzo sat on the lounge, opened the bottle, and poured some lotion into the palm of his hand. His strong fingers glided over her shoulders, making her muscles jump with the feel of his big, powerful hands. She sighed. "Oh, that feels so good."

He stroked lower on her back, his fingers brushing under the elastic of her bikini, lingering before he pulled his hand away. Now both his hands moved over the backs of her thighs and down to her ankles.

What was happening to her? She was so wet, and the burning sensation between her legs felt stronger the more he rubbed the lotion over her. She rolled over onto her back, lifting to recline on one elbow. She bent one knee, shielding her eyes from the sun with her other hand. Her lips parted.

Lorenzo jumped up from the chaise and handed her the bottle. "You can do the rest."

"Thank you." Her voice was just a whisper. "Will you have time for a swim before you go back to the bridge?" Zaps of heat flowed through her body, and the sweet burning between her legs intensified with the way he looked at her.

"Would you like that?" His voice felt like a gentle caress.

"Yes, very much." She couldn't contain her smile.

"I'll change and be right back." His husky voice sent a jolt of pleasure through her body.

∾

WHEN HAVE I ever taken time during the day for a swim? It's the added at-sea days, more relaxing. That's why. Not because she's here in that yellow scrap of material barely covering her cute butt. He'd been jealous when she danced with that man, and his hands had cupped her buttocks. Lorenzo had forced himself to keep his hands on her waist when they'd danced. His palms itched to travel over her bare skin, to feel the satin smoothness.

Applying the sunscreen to her back was torture. When his hand had brushed along her softness, and the tips of his fingers had slipped under the elastic, he'd had to stop. He moved to her legs before he abused her brother's trust in him and broke all the rules he lived by. His father's words from ten years ago rang in his ears. *You are without honor. You have disgraced the DiMarco name. You are not my son.*

Right now, Lorenzo had to calm down before he could go out and join Francesca. One look at him and she would know how much he wanted her. He decided not to wear a speedo but chose a looser pair of swim trunks. He stepped out onto the balcony.

She was already in the pool. Her barely covered breasts swayed in the water. He hopped into the long and narrow pool, dunking himself. When he came up, he shook his head, sending drops of water around him. Francesca giggled as she swam away. Lorenzo swam a few laps, and his control returned. He stood at the shallow end of the pool, his arms outstretched along the deck. She turned and swam to him. Her blond hair floated around her, and water clung to her long, thick eyelashes. "This is so nice. I've never had a private pool all to myself."

"It does have its rewards. Sometimes I'll come out here at midnight for a swim."

She climbed out of the pool in that yellow bikini and sat on the ledge. He followed sitting next to her.

She swirled her feet in the water.

"On a different subject. Did that couple ever bother you?" He needed to know.

She stopped moving her feet, and her head snapped in his direction. "I thought we settled that. No, I felt uncomfortable around them, more so because I'm not naive...well actually, after you said... I understood what was implied."

"What do you think they were saying?" He quirked his brow.

Her azure gaze was direct. "You said that they were swingers and I told you. They wanted to have sex with me—all of us together—isn't that like an orgy? That's not my thing. I was turned off by the whole idea. They could do whatever they want. I'm not judging, but not for me or anyone I would date."

She would hate me for my lifestyle. "Mmmm, yes, to each their own." He changed the subject. "Are you seeing anyone back home?"

She swayed into his shoulder. "You asked that before, at dinner the other night. Remember? Anyway, no, not right now. My last boyfriend was a dream killer."

"How so?"

"Everything had to be his way or the highway. He wanted me to get a—as he put it—practical job. I want more than that. I want a career. We never went out dancing or did any fun things, not even going to a movie. He wanted to stay home and have me serve him. No eating out, ever. He tried to manipulate me and wasn't happy that Stella and I are opening a boutique."

"It sounds as if he didn't want a serious relationship. You deserve better than that. You're independent. That's a good thing, and you should have whatever you desire. Always go for your dreams. Don't let anyone stifle you."

"Yes, my thoughts exactly." She stood and went to get two towels. Lorenzo rose, and Francesca threw him a towel. She used the other to wrap around herself. Hiding her seductive curves from his view. Her blond hair began to dry into waves around her shoulders and down her back.

"Do you have to go back to work? I really had a nice time with you."

She looked sad, and he wanted nothing more than to stay with her, but he couldn't forget his responsibilities. "Yes. I have to be on the bridge. What will you do?"

She pouted, pushing her lower lip out. "I'm going to have dinner in the dining room, and then go to the show with some of my tablemates."

He toweled himself dry before he said, "I get off at nine. Come back to the cabin. We can have a drink and dance here under the stars. Just the two of us."

Joy transformed her features. "Like the other night? I would love that. Zo... do you remember... when you kissed me?"

He wanted desperately to pull her into his arms and do just that. "I never kissed you, Imp."

"Yes. Don't you remember, for my tenth birthday?"

His grin spread. He held her hand in his and bent to place a kiss on it. His thumb rubbed her wrist before turning her palm up to kiss the center. His gaze held hers.

"Mmmm, you didn't do that when I was ten. Kiss my palm like that, I mean… I like it."

"You're older now. Back then, I would have been accused of all sorts of things."

"Now I can accept a kiss like a woman who knows what she wants." Her gaze held a spark of desire in the blue depths, and she swayed toward him. He didn't misread her desire.

CHAPTER 6

Francesca would have had to be dead not to get that message. When he'd turned her hand over, his black eyes held hers as his lips touched the center. She felt the tip of his tongue brush her palm, and her heart fluttered. Her body flooded her with a burning desire. She was definitely alive.

"I have to change and go to a staff meeting."

"What? Oh, yes, okay… I'll get ready for dinner with my friends." She hurried to her bedroom. *I didn't misunderstand him. The feel of his tongue on my palm burned in my core. I know he wants me as much as I desire him.*

Francesca rushed through dinner with her friends. She called Lorenzo to say she wasn't going to the show, she'd rather spend the time with him. "I'll be waiting." His voice vibrated through her body.

Her heart pounded with anticipation as she ran back to the cabin. When she unlocked the door, she saw Lorenzo standing by his desk in a black silk shirt, the first four buttons open, revealing his muscular chest covered with a smattering of black hair. He wore black slacks, with a belt that had a double G gold buckle, and leather loafers. So very tall and handsome. His chiseled features and black hair with a slight wave cut short at the nape. *I want to memorize him.*

She couldn't keep the excitement from her voice. "I hurried through dinner, not even waiting for dessert."

"We can definitely have dessert here in the cabin. A lava cake perhaps." His husky voice made her throb.

"Have you eaten dinner yet?"

"Yes, in the officer's mess. Would you like a drink?"

"Mmmm, what do you suggest? I'm not a drinker, other than wine, and that one piña colada when I boarded." She went to sit on the couch.

"I have just the thing." He walked over to the bar, retrieved a bottle of Pellegrino from the fridge and a bottle of Pino Grigio from the wine cooler. He mixed her drink, then poured a healthy helping of brandy into a snifter. He brought her the white wine spritzer and sat next to her. "Here's to a fun vacation."

She touched her glass to his. "Thank you. You have made it that for me."

"I'm happy to be here with you."

She'd never asked if he was in a relationship, and now she didn't know how to ask. She took a deep breath. "Lorenzo, is there anyone... you know, like... someone special in your life?"

"You want to know if I'm committed?"

"Yes. I remember how the girls always chased you."

"Were you jealous?" She heard his teasing tone.

"I was ten! Yes, I had a crush on you... I dreamt of you and pretended..." Francesca put her glass down on the coffee table. She couldn't tell him. She lowered her gaze and clasped her hands together. At his groan, she lifted her eyes to his.

"Don't be uncomfortable Francesca. It's normal to fantasize and wonder when you're young. But as for your question…" His brow lifted. She couldn't take her eyes from his lips, her mouth dried. "There is no one, Imp."

She stared into his eyes, her voice only a whisper. "I'm glad."

He stood, outstretching his hand. "Dance with me."

She lay her small hand on his. Lorenzo closed his long fingers over hers and bowed. She stood. "But there's no music… I—"

"No worries." Lorenzo hummed a Sicilian love song that she recognized. She lifted her hands to his broad shoulders, and he slipped an arm around her waist and one across her back, holding her to him. Then he swayed to the music, taking her with him.

His scent enveloped her as his strong arms held her. Francesca couldn't stop thinking of Lorenzo and the feel of his body. So much more a man than she remembered. At ten, she was a child wishing she were older. She'd dreamt of him, jealous of the women he dated.

When he suddenly left Sicily, she seldom thought of him. After he left Palermo, she hadn't heard much about him until her brother and Giorgio went to Harvard. They bought motorcycles and rode cross country to meet Lorenzo at the California Maritime Institute. She stopped fantasizing about him and never thought to see him again. Then this cruise came about. Did she subconsciously hope she would see him? Yes!

She swayed against him, laying her head on his chest. "Mmmm, this is so nice."

He stopped moving, and she lifted her head from his chest to look up into his eyes.

Lorenzo couldn't stop himself. She was beautiful, blue eyes flashing her desire. *It is madness to want to kiss her, do more than hold her soft body.* He cupped her face with his hands and tasted her mouth for the first time.

She parted her lips. *To kiss her forever would never be long enough.* His tongue slid into her mouth. Lorenzo held her as she wrapped her silky arms around him his neck, pressing her breasts into him. Her petite body was all he ever wanted. Her tongue timidly touched his, and he reminded himself to go slow. She rose on her toes, offering herself to him. He knew the signs of a woman's passion, and now with Francesca, he would break every rule he imposed on himself.

Lorenzo had to taste her skin, needing to make love with her. She sighed, and he kissed her neck as his hand moved along her waist, up her torso to hold a perfect breast. She held his head to her, hardly breathing. He ran his thumb back and forth over the nipple. The peak swelled under his thumb, and he used his other arm to hold her tighter against his body.

Francesca kissed him, and he whispered in her ear, "Are you sure?"

She wrapped her arms tighter around his neck, leaning into him. Caressing his shoulders, before her hands met at the nape of his neck. "Yes. I've fantasized and dreamt of you," she sighed and tugged his head down to her parted lips.

She teased his lips, then pressed hers more firmly to his, kissing, sucking, nibbling. A kiss that was hot and full of desire. He slanted his mouth over hers and slid his tongue into her mouth. He was lost in the moment, in a kiss that would never end. Lorenzo knew that he would remember the taste of Francesca with his dying breath.

She backed out of his arms, her lips swollen from his hungering kisses. She smiled and pulled her blouse from the waistband of her skirt. Her fingers flew over the pearl buttons. Lorenzo didn't spend a lot of time undressing women; they were usually naked by the time he arrived.

The anticipation of seeing Francesca naked dried his mouth as his dick pressed against his zipper. He helped her rid herself of the silk. He drank in her perfect round breasts encased in the sheer powder-blue bra. He couldn't take his eyes from her puckered areolas as he brushed the satin straps down her arms to her elbows and unfastened her bra.

"Oh yes," she gasped, pressing her naked breasts into his chest.

Not bothering to unbutton the last few buttons, he ripped his shirt open. Lorenzo had to feel her, skin to skin. He dragged her against him, holding her to him. Francesca's hard and excited nipples dug into his chest. His lips brushed against hers, as he said, "Tell me to stop." Raising his mouth from hers, he gazed into her blue eyes.

"No, I don't want you to stop."

"Oh, Francesca." He kissed her brow, the tip of her nose, her lips, her neck, her shoulder, and then across to her breast. He felt the weight of her excited orb, the pink nipple diamond hard. He lowered his head to caress the extended bud with his tongue. Francesca arched her back as he sucked her into his mouth. She panted, and he moved to treat her other breast with the same passion. Francesca curled into his body.

Lorenzo lifted her into his arms and strode to his bedroom. "Zo..." He gently laid her across his bed. She was the only woman he'd ever taken here. He wanted to memorize her seductive curves. Her blond hair spread out in waves over his pillow. Slowly, he unzipped her skirt, sliding the fabric past her hips and down her legs. She lay there with only her sheer panties on. He liked clean-shaven pussy if he had to go down on a woman. But the tuft of blond hair between her legs sent fire racing through his body.

Finally, he had her under him; all he wanted was to give her pleasure.

"Lorenzo, I need you," Francesca moaned.

He wanted to go faster. Her words wiped away all his doubts. Her age. Her brother's friendship. His choice of life-style. Francesca's skin was honey gold from the sun, and he needed to taste her, feel the texture of her nipples, first one and then the other again. He cupped a breast, bringing his mouth down to capture her excited nipple.

"Oh *si, si,* Zo."

Never before had he felt so excited and satisfied by a woman's shudders.

He kissed under her breasts, down her torso before he nuzzled the inside of her thigh. He dropped to his knees and tugged her to the foot of the bed. Her scent filled his head. Lavender and woman's desire floated around him. He slid her panties from her legs, making sure she was comfortable before nudging his shoulders between her toned legs.

His dick throbbed at the sight of her sweet pussy covered with a strip of blond curls, more exciting than what he believed. All he wanted was to take her into his mouth, kiss her center before he spread her. Lorenzo slipped a finger into her; she was so wet. "Francesca," he groaned, swirling his finger in her depths.

She moaned. "Lorenzo, I've… no one has ever—"

"Do you want me to stop?" He would die if she said yes. He looked up her lethal body. Francesca's blond hair spread around her and the blue of her eyes grew deeper like the depths of the ocean.

She groaned, "No, don't stop."

His mouth watered. *I'm the first man to taste her.* His dick swelled to bursting against his zipper. He smiled, kissing her inner thigh as it quivered against his lips. "Francesca, you're going to love this, wait and see." He slid his tongue along her seam, kissing her center. His hand stroked up her torso, cupping a breast, and his gaze found hers. The blue eyes wide. He slowly slid his tongue into her.

Her gasp filled the cabin, and he controlled himself, not spreading her or thrusting his tongue in just yet. He licked her sweet pussy, before the tip of his tongue moved on her clit. Watching Francesca, he needed to make this first experience all for her.

She lifted her hips up to him, and Lorenzo gently spread her with his thumbs. She was bewitching, all pink and glistening with her desire. He traced her inner folds with his tongue.

She moaned, "Oh, Zo, I never knew."

He went slowly savoring her. Dipping his tongue into her sweet center thrusting a handful of times before he circled her clit with the tip of his tongue. Her moaning grew deeper with her breath, and he slipped his hands under her buttocks. Keeping her spread with his thumbs, he began again. Going deeper with his tongue, flicking back and forth.

"Ahh, ahhh, ahhh." Her fingers stroked his head. "I, *Santo Cielo*, Zo."

He wanted her to come on his tongue. He lifted her to his mouth as she spread her thighs wider for him. He reached into her, licking and thrusting before he circled her clit again. When he sucked that excited bud, she screamed her pleasure. He thrust his tongue into her wet heat, wanting to feel her shudders as she convulsed in her climax.

"Oh, *Dio mio*," she panted. Her hands fell away from his head, and the tension left her honey-tanned legs. He kept her thighs on his shoulders, giving her time to recover. He wanted to enjoy her as no other woman, and he needed to do it all again. He kissed her abdomen before resting his chin on her mound. "Again?" She was beautiful, blond hair a tangle of curls spread out on the mattress. The flush of her orgasm spread over her breasts. Francesca's beautiful breasts rising and falling with her breath. Her torso and the indent of her tiny waist, her thighs spread over his shoulders. He could stay like this forever.

"I never experienced anything so wonderful... yes. Can I?"

"Oh yes, you can," he said.

This time, he pressed the heels of her feet on his shoulders, happy to have all of her exposed to his lips and tongue. She curled her body toward his mouth, and he felt the tension of her excitement. She moaned when he opened his mouth, taking her pussy, sucking her flesh.

Francesca stroked her fingers through his hair, and pressing her heels into his shoulders, she lifted her hips to him. He liked her eagerness and thrust his tongue into her heated core. She held his head, panting, "Ahh, ahhh, Zo."

Lorenzo watched her. He lifted her buttocks and with his thumbs, opened her sweet flesh, licking and sucking the sensitive folds before he lashed at her clit. "Oh God, Zo. Yes, please."

He sucked her clit into his mouth before thrusting a finger into her. Lorenzo swirled his finger in her wet heat, feeling the pulsing of her orgasm, he thrust his finger into her again and again, keeping his tongue on her clit. She fell back, and her legs slipped off his shoulders. Her wild gasps filled him with male satisfaction he'd never experienced before. Watching her in the throes of ecstasy, all he wanted was to give her more pleasure.

He stood, and Francesca shimmied up the bed while he unzipped his pants. Taking the condom from his pocket, he dropped his pants and underwear to the floor. He was quick rolling the condom on and lying over her.

Francesca lifted her arms to hold him. "Lorenzo, that was wonderful." She stroked his back.

Lorenzo kissed her lips and with one knee, he nudged her

legs apart. He moved and stopped at her entrance. He held a tender breast in his hand. The nipple stabbing into his palm, he kissed her other breast, sucking her excited peak into his mouth. He pressed his hips forward and entered her that first tiny bit, heaven on earth. No one felt better than her. Ever.

Francesca ran her hands over his shoulders and back up his neck to bury her fingers in his hair. She moaned, "Zo, oh Zo." Sliding her hands over his back and then down his arms, she tipped her hips up to him.

Her eagerness zapped his control. She was tight, oh so tight. He couldn't wait to be surrounded by her heat. He pushed into her slick passage.

How could he have missed the signs? He was speechless in his surprise. She was a virgin. He kept still deep in her tight core.

"Francesca! I didn't know. Did I hurt you?" He knew he had. He kissed her brow, her closed eyelids, her cheeks.

A half frown, half smile on her lips. "No. Yes, but no more pain; only you deep in me." She opened her eyes, and her blue gaze held his. She smiled up at him before she kissed his jaw. "You really do feel so good."

He groaned. "I'll go slow. Tell me if I hurt you."

"Can you kiss me again?"

"*Si, per sempre.*" Yes, always. He swooped down and took her mouth with his, gentle back and forth at first until she lifted her legs around his hips, the heel of one foot gliding over his butt. She darted her tongue into his mouth to twine with his. He moved in her sweet, tight heat. Loving the precious gift she gave him.

CHAPTER 7

Francesca saw his surprise and how quickly Lorenzo recovered. His lips gently swept over her brow, her cheeks, before she asked him to kiss her. His sensuous lips brushed over hers, tugging her bottom lip into his mouth, touching his tongue to the center.

He stretched her, and she relaxed around him. Francesca never wanted to forget how good he felt in her. She melted as the flame of desire reignited with his gentle thrusts, until the pleasure built up, and she forced him to go faster and deeper.

He kissed her over and over again. There was nothing but this man and his body over her, in her, giving pleasure. The room vanished, nothing but him looking at her. Into her soul. *I love you. I love you.* Her mind chanted as the ecstasy built.

Her abdomen clenched, and his lips caught her deep moan. She had never experienced anything as wonderful as the fullness of him deep inside her. Her head fell back on his pillow, and she arched her back, rubbing her tender breasts into the silky black hair of his chest. He kissed her throat, her collarbone. She felt the wave of her orgasm overtake her, and he pumped deep into her core.

"*Si, Bellissima*, you feel so good coming around my dick." She blushed at his words, but he did feel good deep in her as she experienced this different orgasm as wonderful as the previous ones he'd given her with his mouth. She gasped as she pulsed around his hard shaft. He pulled her hips, burying himself to the hilt. His powerful body was covered in a sheen of mist.

Lorenzo shouted, and the power of his orgasm erupted in her. His hot, ragged breath hissed in her ear. Lorenzo held her tighter for a heartbeat before he lifted his weight off her. He kissed the tip of her nose and rolled off her.

"Oh Lorenzo, I'm… glad it was you."

"I'll be right back," he said in a low, distant voice.

Did I do something wrong? He just left the bed. His naked backside was all she saw. A chill ran up her spine, spreading through her body. She hurried out of the bed, searching for her bra and panties. She found her skirt flung to the side of the bed.

"What are you doing?"

His deep voice startled her. She straightened, no longer comfortable with him seeing her naked. Lorenzo had put on a pair of silk boxers and held a towel in one hand.

She hugged her skirt to her breasts. Trying for bravado, her chin jutted out. "You left, so I was going back to my room." She lowered her eyes as humiliation seeped into her bones.

He padded over to her. "Francesca, I went to dispose of the condom. I don't want you to leave. I want to hold you in my arms, cherish you."

Heat burst into her cheeks. "Condom? Oh, of course. My bad."

She stood unsure of what to do, and Lorenzo stood in front of her. He lifted her chin with his closed hand, his thumb rubbing against her bottom lip. "One day, I hope you will tell me where you learned all these very American expressions." He dropped the washcloth and towel on the nightstand. Lorenzo bent and kissed her, tugging her skirt from her hands, dropping it back onto the floor. Then he lifted her into his arms. He laid her in the center of the bed. She saw the faint streak of blood on the sheet. She swallowed and closed her eyes.

"I'm sorry I hurt you. I brought a cool towel for you. May I?" She nodded. He ran the cloth over her mound, soothing and cleaning her.

His gentleness and care of her melted her heart. Then they lay in each other's arms, and she leaned against his massive chest. The steady beat of his heart thrummed against her cheek. Her fingers ran through the smattering of silky black hair on his chest. She'd never felt anything so satisfying. He was a mass of muscles, and Francesca marveled at the hardness of his sculpted body. *He really does look like the statutes back home. He could have posed for Michelangelo's David.*

She loved the way his fingers slid through her hair, and he held her wrapped in his muscular arms. "You want to know how I learned English with an American accent?"

"Yes, Imp, tell me."

"Stella has a few cousins around our age who live in Brooklyn, and we video chat with them all the time. They taught us some of the expressions."

She listened to his deep laugh rumble in his chest before it exploded into the room.

He half-tugged her under him, kissing her lips, and she knew that she needed him to make love to her again.

"Zo."

He pushed her hair back from her face. "This is uncharted

territory for me. Francesca, you have to tell me if you can again. I don't want to hurt you in any way."

She loved the sea captain in him and his nautical terms. Lifting her arms to loop around his neck. "Your care of me is wonderful. Kiss me… I want you again."

He groaned and swooped down, taking her lips with tender sweeps of his. She opened her mouth, and he held her while his tongue played with hers. She needed to feel the pleasure he gave her again. More than that, she wanted to touch him, explore his muscular body. She tore her mouth from his, panting. "Zo, I'm…I want to look at you, touch you… do to you… what you did to me."

His groan confused her, but he wiggled his brows, and the smile on his sensuous lips told her he wanted that too. Lorenzo lay on his back, folding his arms behind his head as he rested against the headboard. He was gorgeous in his masculinity.

She caught her breath. Maybe it was better she hadn't seen him before. *He's huge. I can't believe he fits in me. Every part of his glorious body is covered in muscles.*

"I don't know how long I can be still, Imp, but go ahead."

She stared at his handsome face, now covered with evening stubble. His full lips soft yet firm, masculine. She touched the bow of his bottom lip with her finger. He nipped it, and she suppressed a laugh. Then she moved so that her fingers trailed down the cords of muscles in his neck before moving over his chest. She stopped and looked into his eyes. The smoldering fire in the black depths startled her, but then she grew brave. Bending over, she kissed his chest, circled his flat nipple, before moving to the other. In a similar way that he did to her.

Lorenzo caressed her head before his hand moved down her back. She trailed kisses down the thin line of black hair over his torso, lower and lower before she realized his erection had grown larger. She lost her nerve, not sure what to do.

"Imp, one day, I would love nothing more than you to take me in your mouth… but not now. Come here and let me love you." He leaned over and urged her onto her back.

She was grateful that he understood her hesitance. This, although wonderful, was new to her. Lorenzo brushed a kiss on her brow, whispering in her ear how much he wanted her before touching her earlobe with his tongue. She shivered in his embrace.

"Soon, you'll be doing more than shivering. Soon, you'll be screaming your pleasure." His deep sexy voice floated around her.

He didn't give her a chance to answer as he crushed her lips to his. She opened to him, and he slid his tongue in to spar with hers.

Lost in his kiss, his taste, his male strength covering her body, Francesca held his head to her, needing the kiss to never end, but then he slid his mouth along her neck, down one shoulder, before he reached her breast. *Oh, Dio mio, his mouth is so hot and his tongue. Oh yes, yes.* He circled the areola, before nipping at her breast. Her nipple hardened, needing his kisses. Lorenzo moved to the valley between her breasts and on to the other breast. He lashed at her nipple. "Oh, Zo, I can't believe how you make me feel."

Kneeling between her legs, he didn't answer her but reached to his bedside table and retrieved a square foil packet.

Where did that come from?

He ripped open the packet and rolled the protection onto his erection. She felt the heat rise into her cheeks and her eyes round. *How could that fit on him?*

He leaned over her, his hands on either side of her shoulders. "*Bellissima*, I'm going to make you feel so much more. You tell me if your body needs to rest."

She nodded. Then he was at her entrance, and all she could think of was the exquisite pleasure and the fullness as he thrust into her. His muscular abdomen inches above hers, she could see where they were joined, and she felt him inside her, so snug and good. He lifted above her and locked his elbows, moving deeper. The feel of his steel-hard flesh in her drove her to arch her body. "*Bellissima*, you are so tight around my dick, and your body spread out before me is driving me crazy. Lift your legs around my hips. I have to move."

She did, and the sensation added to the intimate embrace. He slid out and thrust in, then slid out further before pushing in deeper, making her newly awakened nerve endings crave the deep thrusts. She gasped as his erection stroked a spot that felt so good.

"You like that, Francesca?"

Her back arched. "Yes, that felt wonderful. Do it again."

He did more than once before he lowered his body so that he could kiss her. She slipped her hands around his neck and locked her ankles over his waist as she moved her hips to hold him deep in her.

Heat zinged through her body as one pulse led to another and another, faster as wave after wave washed over her. She did scream then, but he caught most of it with his lips. The little that escaped were moans of pleasure.

Lorenzo's heart beat against her chest, and his scent, so masculine, filled her. She felt the shift of his rock-hard muscles under her hands, her fingers curling as he came deep in her body. She smiled at the wonder of it all. Lorenzo, her childhood crush was above her, his hair a tangled mess from her fingers. He kissed her before he whispered in her ear, "I'm going to the ensuite for a moment."

"I won't leave."

"Good, the night is not over by any means."

She rolled to her side in the bed and waited for him to come back to her. As he walked toward her, with each step he took, his muscles shifted and stretched. Lorenzo lay against the pillows and pulled her into his arms. Happily, Francesca lay against him, her fingers drawing patterns on his chest before following the thin line of dark hair over his torso. He held her hand still. "I have no control with you. I think it will cause you pain if we make love again."

She rubbed her leg against his longer ones. "I only feel pleasure, unimaginable pleasure in your arms."

"I have been around the world more than once, and I've never experienced anything like what I feel with you, Francesca, *tesoro mio*."

"Mmmm, Zo, you make me feel treasured. You've made all my dreams and more come true."

Lorenzo held her in his arms, and they dosed for a while. Then he gave her his shirt to wear while they went into the living room. From the bar, he brought her a panino of prosciutto and one for himself. Then he poured them each a glass of wine. Lorenzo pulled her onto his lap, and they ate and laughed. "I can't believe how wonderful you make me feel."

He kissed her neck. "It's never been better for me, Imp. Never."

It was almost dawn when they fell asleep in each other's arms. She woke up to the gentle brush of his lips on her shoulder. His knees tucked under her legs, and one strong arm draped over her waist. "I have to go to the bridge, do my rounds. You stay in bed if you like."

She rolled over in his powerful arms, kissing his warm lips. "Mmm, that sounds wonderful. But can't you... maybe make love to me before you go?"

"I would like nothing more than to introduce you to morning sex, but the faster I go, the sooner I'll be back, and we can make love all day."

She pushed at his broad chest. "Then why are you still in bed?"

Lorenzo laughed as he sat up and then threw his legs over the side of the bed and sauntered naked into the ensuite. She heard the shower turn on and lay in bed, reliving each moment of last night.

He was dressed when he came out of the ensuite. "I'll ask Mario to bring you breakfast. You can do nothing but rest today."

"Thanks. Can you ask him to wait an hour? I want to shower and then I'm going to sit on the balcony, maybe swim, and read my book."

He kissed her on the cheek before he left.

Francesca stretched from her fingers to her toes before she got out of his bed. Picking up her clothes, she looked at the rumpled sheets. The streak of blood now dry caught her eye, and she decided to remove the sheets, not wanting Mario to see anything. Then she went into her room to shower and put on a bathing suit. Surprisingly, her muscles didn't ache; she felt invigorated.

Lorenzo walked out onto the balcony carrying a tray with two cups of cappuccino and two cornetti, one cornetto filled with hazelnut cream for her. He sat next to her. "I thought you wouldn't mind if I brought you breakfast. Would you like to go to the movie? I've arranged to have the theater all to ourselves this afternoon."

"I love it. The whole movie to ourselves."

"Yes, Imp. I'll come back at two so we can go."

"Okay."

Mario had come in to tidy up the cabin, and Francesca sat in the shade on the balcony, reading. She ordered a smoothie for lunch and then changed into white pants and a cropped purple top for the movie. She'd applied some makeup and black eyeliner, making cat eyes. Then she piled her hair on top of her head in a messy bun and slipped her feet into flat white sandals.

Lorenzo walked into the cabin just as Francesca stepped out of her bedroom. "You look beautiful."

She felt her cheeks stain with a blush. He took her in his arms and kissed her, then slipped his arm around her waist as they walked to the elevator. "I have everything set up. There is buttered popcorn, and just you and me in the main theater." His thumb stroked her bare skin below the cropped top.

"Which movies do they have?"

"You'll get to choose what you want to watch." The elevator stopped and he took her hand in his walking down a corridor to the theater.

A security guard stood at the side entrance. "Captain DiMarco, sir," he said as he opened the door for them.

Lorenzo led her to the front row and the two center seats. He had everything waiting on a low table. "Yummy, the popcorn smells so good, and we have drinks too."

He handed her the tub of warm popcorn. "Yes, Imp. I hope you don't mind, but I've selected the first movie."

"No. I'm happy to just be here with you."

He spoke into a small walkie talkie, and the lights gradually dimmed to total darkness. Her eyes adjusted and the movie began. It was a rom com she'd wanted to see but never had.

She fed him bites of popcorn, and he licked the butter from the tips of her fingers. He put his arm around her shoulders, and they watched the movie, laughing at the jokes. She rested her head on his shoulder. "I didn't know you liked chick-flicks."

His laugh rumbled through his chest before bursting out. "I've never, but with you, it's fun. Want to watch another?"

"Yes, please and thank you."

"You choose this time," he said, brushing his lips on her brow.

"Okay, how about this one?"

Lorenzo told the projectionist which one to put on. He kissed her brow again as they sat in the dark theater waiting for the movie to begin. When the movie ended he whispered in her ear, "Let's go back to the cabin... take a shower together."

She sat up. "Really, a shower."

"Yes, Imp."

She tugged his hand. "Hurry. I've heard that making love in the shower is great."

"Hmm, is that so? Let's not disappoint." Lorenzo lifted her over his shoulder.

Francesca shrieked. "What are you doing?"

"Hurrying," he said as his hand caressed her buttocks. When he reached the exit, he bent so she could stand. "It wouldn't look good to see the captain running with a sexy woman over his shoulder. You'll have to walk the rest of the way."

"We can speed walk," she said, taking his hand.

"Yes, let's do that." He tugged her along to the elevator. Once the doors slid closed, he thoroughly kissed her, only pulling apart to walk into his cabin. He held her against the closed door, kissing her as his fingers unfastened the button on the waist of her white pants. She wrapped her arms around his neck. The sound of her zipper opening throbbed through her core. His hand fit snug inside her panties, and one long finger ran along her seam.

"Oh, Zo." Francesca pulled her blouse up and tore her mouth from his long enough for her to pull it over her head.

His sensuous lips landed on hers again as his finger slid into her core. She shuddered at the pleasure.

Her fingers trembled as she unbuckled his belt, then unbuttoned his shirt, pulling the tails out of his waistband. "I don't think we're going to make it to the shower," he said against her lips.

She groaned and ran her leg along his muscled shank to his waist. He thrust his finger into her stroking her folds a few times as he bent his head to suck her nipple through the lace of her bra. The tip of his finger touched her excited clit. "Oh… Zo… Zo, yes. That feels so good."

He lifted his head from her breast. "Your pussy drenched my finger and is begging to come just like this."

"Yes." She wrapped her arms around his neck, digging her heel into his lower back. His finger circled her clit. Her head fell back. "Oh God, yes. Do that again, yes, yes."

Then he thrust two fingers into her heated vagina and slid his thumb back and forth over her clit. She was wild, her hips rocking into him, taking his fingers deeper into her. "Oh!"

"Yes, *tesoro*. I feel you coming."

She panted into his neck, mewling her pleasure. When her pulsations stopped, he lifted her, holding the globes of her buttocks as she wrapped her legs around his waist, and he walked into the ensuite. "Shower sex or tub sex?"

"Mmmm, shower sex." Her voice sounded euphoric and faraway to her ears.

He stood her next to the marble and glass-enclosed shower before he turned on the water. Lorenzo stripped himself, then he unhooked her bra and slid her pants and panties down her legs. He dragged her into the shower, the warm spray feeling good on her sensitized body. He lathered a washcloth. "I'm going to run this cloth over every inch of you."

"Only if I can do the same to you." She reached up touching the planes of his cheeks and running her fingertips over his sensuously sculpted lips before she stroked her hands over his broad shoulders and down his arms. Taking his hand that held the washcloth she brought it to her breasts.

"Oh yes, Imp, show me what you want."

Shower sex was better than Francesca could ever imagine. Sliding the soapy cloth over her body Lorenzo rinsed her. "Now for the best part," he said and knelt, dragging her to his mouth. Heat flared through her and she pulsed with excitement as his tongue slipped into her core. Her fingers tangled in his hair while he took his time licking each of her hidden folds.

"Oh, *Dio mio si, si*," she moaned when he sucked her clit.

Leaning against the shower wall, she pressed her open palms on the marble for support. Lorenzo guided her leg over his shoulder. His tongue circled her clit, slipping into her center, then back to her clit, sucking her into his mouth. Fire coursed through her body. She wanted him to never stop. And at the same time, she wanted to come right now, so she could experience everything he could make her feel. The spray of the shower couldn't cool her. She looked at him and recognized the desire in his eyes. She groaned when the first pulse of an orgasm snuck into her. Tipping her head back, she stroked his hair with one hand. His wicked tongue lashed at her clit. Francesca was on fire. "Please, Zo," she said and arched her body.

He sucked her clit and thrust a finger into her. He'd been gentle until she begged him to make her come. A second finger slid into her, thrusting, scissoring, stroking her. Francesca bit the corner of her bottom lip as pleasure sizzled through her body. Her fingers tangled in his wet hair pulling Lorenzo closer. She screamed leaning against him, holding his head to her. His fingers were deep in her as the waves of her orgasm crashed through her body. *"Dio, dio*, ahhh… I love shower sex."

He stood and caught her up in his arms before she slid down the wall to the marble floor. She traced his sensuous lips. Lips that had just brought her so much pleasure. They were tender as he kissed her. She had to do what he did to her. "Zo, let me… touch you… the same way." Her hand glided over the washboard abs of his body. Francesca reached for his erection. Sliding to her knees, she looked up his tall beautiful body. He'd braced his feet apart in the captain's stance, his erection jutting out of the patch of black hair. She took him in her hand. Surprised that her fingers were steady, although she wasn't sure exactly what to do.

Her friends had talked about this, telling her that men wanted this more than fucking. They only went down on you so you would do this for them. She found that difficult to believe with the way Lorenzo acted. He always looked out for her pleasure, making her come more than once before he came. Even in her innocence, she knew he made sure she would climax first, sometimes more than once or together.

Her multiple orgasms were shared passion, and she felt it in her heart that there weren't any ulterior motives. Now, she would do what he wanted, even though he never asked and actually stopped her more than once. "Francesca, only if you are sure—"

She gazed up into his eyes, the shower spray on his back, his torso covered with rivulets of water, one following the thin line of hair to his erection. "Yes, I want to… but—"

"We'll go slow… you can stop when you want."

"Zo, I want to."

"Tesoro, you are beautiful. If you're sure then put your lips on the head of my dick." He held his long, thick shaft, and she did as he said. Touching the velvet softness with a kiss before

she opened her lips. "That's nice," he said as he caressed her cheek. Take me into your mouth."

He didn't move, and she leaned forward to do as he said. He lay on her tongue, and she lifted a hand to encircle him. She marveled at how her fingers couldn't meet around him. Francesca tried to circle the head with her tongue. He inched out and then in a little more. He moved in some more and inched out. Each time Lorenzo slid in a little further. Her hand rose to lie on his thigh and he immediately began to pull out. Francesca glided her hand from his thigh up and around to his butt. Lorenzo stayed with just the head of his erection in her mouth. She touched her tongue to the underside.

He groaned, "Yes, right there." She couldn't believe the way his body jumped when the tip of her tongue touched the ridge of flesh. She lashed at that spot over and over again until he gradually pushed in to her mouth. "Just a little more," he panted. Lorenzo pushed her wet hair from her face and caressed her cheek while he pumped in and out of her mouth.

Her mouth was so full of him, she couldn't do more than nod. Instinct alone guided her to caress and cup his balls with her other hand.

"*Tesoro*," he groaned at that and pulled out. He lifted her up to her feet and kissed her. Then Lorenzo used his hand and hers to finish. She'd never felt anything so sexy. His power as he came in an explosion of virile man amazed her. Lorenzo rinsed them before he dried her and himself in two big fluffy towels. He lifted her in his powerful arms and carried her to the bed. Francesca snuggled under the covers, content to be in his arms. Her lids felt heavy. She was so sated she couldn't move. Lorenzo nuzzled her neck. "Francesca, you amaze me." He kissed her brow. "I have to go to the bridge for an hour or two. Why don't you take a nap?"

"Mmmm, a captain's work is never done."

"Or his pleasure. Would you like to go to the French restaurant tonight?"

"Yes, I would love that."

"Dinner at nine, okay?"

"Yes, Zo."

CHAPTER 8

Francesca sat at the bar. She'd pinned her hair up in a sleek bun and was already dressed for dinner in a gold gown when Lorenzo came into the cabin. "I asked Mario what type of martini you liked."

He kissed her cheek before taking a sip of the martini. "Ahh, perfection, just like you. *Tesoro*, you take my breath away with your beauty. Is this gown one of your creations? The fabric looks like liquid gold."

"Yes, I designed it."

"I don't know too much about women's clothing, but from your outfits and designs, I can see you have an exceptional talent, *tesoro*."

"Thank you for saying that. It means a lot coming from you. I wasn't snooping when I saw all of your custom made clothes hanging in your walk-in closet. The designer in me couldn't help but notice."

He smiled before he kissed her brow. "I'm going to change and be right back." When he reappeared, he wore a custom-made tuxedo, not his captain's formal wear. His good looks almost turned her into a puddle at his feet.

Lorenzo slipped her arm through his as they walked to the specialty French restaurant. The maître d' brought them to a secluded area of the exquisite venue. Several intimate sections along the back wall were curtained off for complete privacy. She stepped up into the private area with Lorenzo's hand on the small of her back. The wall of large windows had a breathtaking view of the ocean, dark and mysterious at night. The ship's lights reflected on the water. Lorenzo held out her chair at the intimate table covered in a red damask cloth, similar to the red of the privacy curtain. The maître d' handed them each a menu. "Your waiter will be here shortly. Enjoy your dinner."

"I've ordered champagne and a variety of appetizers, including caviar. I didn't know what you wanted to eat, so just order whatever you wish."

"Good evening mademoiselle, Captain. Oh, pardon me, I mean, monsieur. May I pour the Champaign?"

"Yes."

"I will be back to take your dinner order."

When the waiter left, Francesca leaned in and said, "So, they're going to pretend not to recognize you?"

"Yes, Imp, they are under strict orders to treat me like a guest." Taking her hand, he said, "Tonight, I'm a man enjoying dinner with the most beautiful woman in the world."

Heat and pleasure at his words spread over every part of her body.

Once dinner was over, they strolled along the deck, stopping to gaze up at the stars before they went back to his cabin. In the cabin, he took her in his arms and danced a slow dance with her. The music was very seductive, and Lorenzo took her lips as he held her in his arms. Then she rested her head on his chest.

He whispered in her ear, "Would you like to go for a midnight swim?"

"Naked?"

"Yes."

Francesca slipped the spaghetti straps of her gold gown down her arms as Lorenzo helped her unzip the side enclosure. She gazed up at him as her gown slid down her body to pool at her feet. Taking the pins from her hair, the thick mass cascaded around her shoulders.

"I love that you didn't wear a bra," he said, shrugging out of his tuxedo jacket. He unzipped his pants and toed off his shoes.

Francesca shimmied out of her sexy lace thong. She bent to unfasten the ankle straps on her heels. "My bad, I should have asked first. Will the water be warm enough?"

"I set the pool heater earlier, so it should be perfect for us. Imp, don't bend like that if you want to go for a swim."

The balcony lights were dimmed, and the pool water was turquoise. "Oh you," she giggled. She turned to him and lowered her voice. "You're sure that no one can see or hear us?"

"Yes. You know that there is complete privacy here in my cabin."

"Okay, Zo." Francesca got into the pool. "Ahh, you're right. The water is perfect."

"I always look out for your pleasure."

He looked like a Roman statue, standing there naked. Even in the water, she felt her nipples tighten as she looked at him. Then he got into the pool and came to stand in front of her. She looped her arms around his neck, and he bent to kiss her. As he did, he cupped her buttocks in his big hands and lifted her. Francesca instinctively wrapped her legs around his waist. She angled her head and opened her lips to him. Lorenzo deepened the kiss, his tongue exploring her mouth. He sank under the surface with their mouths locked. When they came up for air, they walked to the edge. He lifted her out of the pool to sit on the towel he'd lay out on the deck.

"Zo?"

"Spread your knees, Imp. I need to taste you and feel you come on my tongue."

She moaned, "Oh, Zo."

Her body gleamed silver in the moonlight. He watched her as she moved her hands a little behind her rounded hips, keeping her arms straight as she leaned back. "You look like a sea nymph, your body all wet from the pool." Her blond hair hung in waves down her back as she closed her eyes. No one had ever excited him the way Francesca did. He'd never had anything more than sex. Nothing more than a biological urge not even lust. Now, Lorenzo knew with every fiber of his being that he was in love with Francesca. It wasn't just the physical act of making love with her. Lorenzo wanted to make her happy, give her all the things she wanted.

"*Tesoro*, spread your knees."

She did, and Lorenzo kissed the inside of one knee before he got between her supple thighs. Her legs quivered, and he bent to place kisses on the inside of one thigh, then the other, moving to the apex. "I love your pussy." He spread her with his thumbs, kissing her center before he licked her. "You like that when I suck on your clit?"

"Yesss, everything you do." Her head tilted back.

"Then you're going to love this. Put your feet on my shoulders and lie back."

She did, and he held her buttocks in his hands, his thumbs pressing her open. He lifted her to his mouth. Lorenzo thrust his tongue into Francesca, tasting her desire. The sweet honey lingered on his tongue as he traced her delicate folds.

Francesca stroked his head, her fingers tangling in his

hair. She pressed her heels into his shoulders. "Oh, *Dio mio*, Zo."

He sucked her clit before he thrust his tongue into her again and again, lingering in all her secret places. He felt a pulse deep in her core, and he licked her again before he circled her clit. Then he thrust his tongue back into her core. He lifted her higher, and her legs spread wider. Her fingernails dug into his scalp. Lorenzo loved how wild she was in her need.

She mewled as she writhed against his mouth. He felt her shudder and then the pulses coming faster and faster as her back arched, and she shattered, coming on his tongue.

Her panting gasps filled the night. Slowly, her breathing returned to normal, and Francesca released her grip on his head. He loved her and how she opened to him. "Mmm, Zo. I'm in heaven."

He didn't answer her; instead, he kissed her center, sliding his tongue in to taste her again. She lifted onto her elbows. "Zo?"

He opened her to his mouth, his tongue once again tracing her delicate pink folds, now swollen with passion, and he couldn't help but make her come again, just like this. "Francesca, are you all right?"

"Is there someplace higher than heaven? Because I've found it with you."

He pushed himself out of the pool and, in one smooth motion, lifted Francesca to lie her on the chaise lounge. "You have brought me there with you. Never have I experienced what I feel with you." Lorenzo shut off the pool light. "We can stay here for a while and watch the moonbeams light a path on the ocean."

In the morning, they lay in his bed. She was asleep with her head in the crook of his neck, her breath tickling his chest hairs. Francesca had snuggled to his side, her arm across his waist, and now one of her legs rode up his thigh. Today, they were going to explore the pleasures of morning sex. Since he didn't spend the night with any of his women this was another thing he hadn't done in years.

Stroking her hair, his fingers combed through the silky length, teasing a curl. Francesca stirred in his arms. "Mmmm, is it morning already? It feels like we just went to bed."

"Are you complaining?"

"Never." Her hand slid along his abdomen, and her arm brushed his flaming erection. Her eyes popped open. "Oh, will you look at that?"

"Yes, all for you." Lorenzo kissed her sleep warm lips. "Turn on your side, *Tesoro*," he said rolling her over.

He took the condom from the foil packet and rolled it on. He snuggled Francesca to him, with her back to his chest he tucked his knees under her. Wrapping his arm over her tiny waist he cupped a breast before his thumb and forefinger rolled it into a stiff peak. Morning spooning, something too intimate and something he never did. He'd never slept through the night with any of the others, but it felt so right with Francesca. He nuzzled her ear. "Do you like that?"

"Yes, so much." Her head fell back onto his shoulder.

"Bring your leg over my hip, *tesoro*." He moved to enter her and slid his hand down her satin smooth torso reaching his finger into her touching her clit.

"Zo, so nice."

"Yes." He kept his strokes shallow in this new position until Francesca came moaning her pleasure. Lorenzo rolled onto his back and tugged her to him. "Ride me, Imp."

Francesca smiled. "Yes, Zo." She lifted herself and took him deep into her, sliding down his shaft. Lorenzo gripped her waist holding her down on his erection. Her hands on his abdomen, she rocked back and forth. "Your pussy feels so tight and wet."

A pink blush stained her cheeks and she closed her eyes. Lorenzo touched her clit.

"Oh yes, I like that," she moaned.

There was no more time for talking. He felt her pulse around him, throwing her head back, her tangle of blond hair brushing his thighs as she cried out. Lorenzo stroked her clit adding pressure. Francesca shuddered and he groaned as they came together in shared bliss. She fell onto his chest. He wrapped his arms around her, kissing her cheek. He pushed her hair off her flushed face. Their bodies damp in the shared climax. He'd never been more content in his life than at this moment holding Francesca in his arms.

She fell asleep and he snuggled her under the covers. He took a quick shower and then left for the bridge. Lorenzo came back in the afternoon, sitting on the couch with her. He opened his laptop, wanting to be near when he worked. She sat, reading a book. He tugged her closer to him while he tapped away on his laptop. Curling her legs under her, she rested her head on his shoulder. "Would you like to go for a walk on the deck?" he asked.

"Yes, I would love to." She slipped her feet into her sandals.

"The bridge deck is restricted to me and the bridge crew." They held hands and strolled outside on the open deck. When they were alone, he held her to him and thoroughly kissed her.

"Zo, I love it here with you."

"Me too, *tesoro mio.*"

They had another pleasant day making love and cuddling. He surprised her with a candle lit dinner and dancing on his balcony. Tomorrow they would arrive at their first port, Hilo.

"I have to go to the bridge. The pilot is coming aboard. We'll be docking soon."

"Okay," she mumbled and stretched. "Can we have breakfast together?"

"Yes, ask Mario to bring it here." He brushed a kiss on her brow before he left. She showered and dressed in a casual outfit of denim jeans cuffed to form capri pants, a white peasant blouse, and white trainers. She laid her straw hat by her purse and waited. Zo had said that once the local authorities cleared the ship, he would make the announcement for the passengers to go ashore. She was meeting her friends for a day of sightseeing.

CHAPTER 9

*L*orenzo walked into his cabin. "Our breakfast is on the balcony. She walked out the sliding doors, and he followed. Francesca took a cup and a pastry, handing them to Lorenzo, then she took her coffee and went to sit.

"Do you have your identification in a safe place?"

She glanced at him, her brows furrowed. "I'm not a child. Of course I do. It's in my back pocket."

"What?" he snapped.

Her voice was full of merriment. She said, "I'm teasing you. It's in my purse, but you deserve that."

"*Tesoro*, I want to keep you safe," he growled.

She reached over and stroked his cheek. "Thank you. I'll be perfectly all right. I'm meeting some of my dinner companions. We signed up for the Volcanoes National Park tour. What will you do today?"

His eyes shifted, and then he shrugged a shoulder. "I have to go into Hilo and take care of something."

"You don't sound so happy about it."

"It's something I have to do. You go have fun. Did you pack sunblock?"

"Yes, and my hat, sunglasses, and a bottle of water." She furrowed her brows again. "Hey, are you my father or my lover?"

Lorenzo pulled her into him, molding her to his hard body before he kissed her. "Always your lover. Tonight, I will prove it to you until you beg me to stop." He swatted her buttocks. "Now go before you miss your excursion." They walked into the living room, his arm around her shoulders.

"You have a good day as well. I'm going to hold you to that promise." She kissed him, then put her hat on her head and grabbed her Never Full. Hurrying from the cabin before the temptation to stay with him won.

Francesca couldn't contain her excitement. On the debarkation deck, she waited in line for her turn to leave the ship. After showing the security guard her identification, she stepped onto the gangway. A photographer from the ship asked her to pose by a decorated life preserver that said Hilo in the middle. She did. Further down the pier, she found her friends.

Hawaiian music played on the dock, and a group of women dressed in hula skirts danced, while others carried leis. They placed one on her and each of her friends.

"I'm so excited," she said to Claire.

"Me too. This is my first time in Hawaii. Hurry, there's our bus," Claire said, pulling Francesca along.

They boarded the minivan for the tour to the lava tubes and Volcanoes National Park. She'd been to Mt. Etna many times and hiked to the summit to watch the sunrise and another time to watch the sunset, but this was definitely different. These mountains weren't snowcapped.

The tour van stopped at an open market so they could buy some souvenirs. She bought Lorenzo a t-shirt. Then she and her friends went to lunch. The restaurant offered outdoor seating with some spectacular views. They were led to a shaded area. The six women looked at the menu and chose some of the local fare. They were going to share and sample the local dishes. She'd never had kalua pork or poi, so they ordered that and some other traditional Hawaiian food.

"Isn't that Captain DiMarco?" one of her companions asked.

Francesca turned to look. Excitement bubbled in her. *Did he come looking for me?* "Where? I don't see him."

"Over the other way. With those two women."

She turned, a smile on her lips. Francesca's brain froze. The two women were both tall brunettes, each holding him around the waist as they walked. They kissed his neck, and his jaw, then took a turn, each kissing him on the mouth.

One of her friends was talking, but it sounded as if she were in a tunnel. Francesca couldn't understand a word any of her friends said. Her mind was blank to English and she doubted she could understand her native Italian. She forced herself to snap out of her fog and swallowed the lump in her throat. She wanted to wipe out the memory of the last few days and this morning.

"Are they from the ship? Are they passengers?"

"I haven't seen them on our ship." Claire said, "Have you, Frankie... Francesca?"

Francesca strove for indifference as she said, "I've never seen them before."

"Well, they look very chummy, don't you think?"

She couldn't take her eyes off Lorenzo and the two beautiful model tall women. She knew without being told that they were lovers. It was in the way they held him, leaned into him.

Her heart sank, and she fought the tears that threatened

to spill out of her. Everything he did with her felt dirty and no longer special.

Francesca said, "I think I want to walk around here for a while before I go back to the ship."

"We can all use a walk after that big lunch. We're about a mile away from the pier; that would be a nice walk to help us digest. Let's go."

Lunch sat like a lead balloon in Francesca's stomach. The lump in her throat was no better. *He knew about swingers because he's one. Kissing those two women right there in public. Mister, I'm very private.*

"Frankie, don't forget your package and your purse."

"Oh, yes, thanks, Claire."

The walk back to the ship was a blur for Francesca. She somehow made it back into his cabin and locked herself in her bedroom, too numb to think and not sure what to do. She heard him come into the cabin and go to his room. Francesca checked the time. *Two hours before we set sail. He will have to be on the bridge soon.* She listened for him and when he left the cabin; she walked out of her bedroom.

In the living room, in a crystal vase on the coffee table, was a bouquet of tropical flowers with birds of paradise and a note with her name in bold letters on the front. **I thought of you all day. I hope you had fun in Hilo. LDM.** *Lorenzo DiMarco or better yet, Liar. Degenerate. Molester of virgins. That's what he is.* She crumpled the note and threw it into the trash can. *He is such a shit. I can't even look at him, never mind stay here with him.*

She tapped her pinky nail on her bottom teeth. *I have just enough money to get home. No... this is my vacay... I'm staying!*

She stomped her foot and marched back to her room, locked the door, and threw herself across the bed. That's when she buried her head in her pillow. Inconsolable sobs racked her body. She went to her ensuite and wet a facecloth with cold water from the tap, pressing it to her eyes. When had she ever cried like that? Never. She showered, grateful she was in her shower and not his where they'd had the most amazing shower sex. Turning off the water, she banged her fist on the shower wall, furious with herself and him. She dried herself and pulled her wet hair up into a ponytail and put on the first thing she grabbed from her closet. She decided to go out to the balcony—she wouldn't look at the pool or the chaise lounge. Francesca hoped the fresh sea breeze would calm her.

ONCE THE SHIP was on course to its next port, Lorenzo handed command over to his second in command. He wanted to find Francesca. For the first time in a long time, he felt liberated and free of his self-imposed sex without commitment existence. The little virgin taught him about love and caring—he'd never reached such heights of pleasure before.

He found her out on the balcony, leaning against the rail, looking out over the water. She changed from the denim jeans, white blouse she wore this morning into a mini dress that caressed the curve of her back and hugged her butt. Her blond hair was tied in a ponytail. Flat sandals on her dainty feet.

He walked up to her. She didn't turn around to look at him. Her voice sounded listless as it carried over the slight breeze. "You never told me that you were a swinger. You lied to me when you said that you were different. Swinging. Is that the correct term? Well, whatever."

He snapped at her. "I never lied to you. I'm very into only you. *You* made me realize that."

Francesca turned to him, her blue eyes flashing. "What

about the two women I saw you with on Hilo? What about that?"

"You saw me?" He took a step closer to her. "Francesca, you misunderstood what you saw. I had to tell them it was over. I bought them lunch, that was all. I can't be with anyone but you from now on. I like vanilla sex when it's with you and only you."

"I don't trust you. You said there was no one special, and you knew all along about Joe and the others. Why didn't you tell me about you and, and—"

His voice rose. "What did you want me to say?"

She didn't look at him. "I would have liked you to tell me the truth. How you really felt about sex, me…and your life choices."

"These past few days with you… for the first time in my life, my heart sang. I like sex with you. I couldn't think of sharing you with anyone, and I don't ever want to be with anyone but you. That's how I feel about sex. I choose you."

"So convenient. And so fast," she huffed.

"You think I can't decide how I feel about you? Do you think I don't know my own feelings?"

"I don't know what to think—you hurt me."

"I'm sorry," his voice gentled. "Believe me, I never meant for you to see me today. Please come inside." He entwined his fingers with hers, and they walked off the balcony and into the living room. He stripped off his shirt and unzipped his pants.

"What are you doing?" Francesca took a step back, away from him.

"What does it look like? I'm going to make love to you until you beg me to stop."

"Lorenzo, I… I'm not sure—

"I'm positive this is right." He snaked his arms around her waist and dragged her into his body. He didn't hide his flaming arousal as he leaned into her lethal body. He pulled her hips against him. "Can you feel how much I want you?"

He marveled that even in her innocence; she was all he wanted and needed. In the shower, her unschooled attempt to give him pleasure was better than any other experience with any woman. She was perfection and ripped apart his belief that he needed more than one woman to satisfy him. That was clearly misguided. He needed Francesca.

Her cheeks were rosy. She didn't answer but parted her glossy lips, her blue eyes pleading with him to kiss her, tipping her face to him in a clear invitation. He held back for a heartbeat, savoring her before his lips descended on her sweet, welcoming ones. Her hands moved up his naked torso to his shoulders, across to his powerful neck. Her fingers played at his nape while she slid her parted lips over his. She darted her tongue into his mouth, and he knew she wanted the same thing he did. He'd taught her about pleasure, and she taught him about love.

Lorenzo hiked her dress up over her hips and slid his hand into the front of her lace panties, sliding a finger into her. She moved her feet apart for him. He kissed her once more before he dropped to his knees, kissing her belly and lower over her abdomen. He slipped her panties down her golden-tanned legs to the living room carpet. He slid his hands up her shapely legs to cup the firm globes of her buttocks before dipping his head. His tongue teased the tuft of blond hair before he found her clit. He licked and circled her clit before he thrust into her heat. He massaged her butt cheeks and licked her until he tasted her desire.

She held his head, her fingers raking through his hair. "Oh, yes."

He tugged her to him, licking her clit again and again. Never before had he needed to satisfy a woman the way he did with Francesca. Her moan excited him. Finding new ways to please her.

Francesca desperately needed what Lorenzo did with his tongue. Holding her to his mouth, he drew erotic patterns over her mound before touching her clit again, burying his tongue into her. *Ah, yes. Dio mio.* Her fingers furrowed through his hair as she held his head to her. His big, powerful hands on her buttocks held her to his mouth.

Her belly tightened at the pleasure of his tongue on her clit, before dipping into her core. A vision of him doing the same thing with the two other women she saw in Hilo froze her. She shook her head, pushing at his broad shoulders. Then she tugged his hands from her buttocks.

She sobbed. "I can't do this."

His gaze held hers. "What do you mean?"

"I can't, not after... I keep thinking of you and the two women I saw you with. I know–"

"You don't know anything," Lorenzo spat out before he stood, towering over her. Running his fingers through his tousled black hair. "I didn't tell you because this is not something I'm proud of sharing with you. I'm sorry you saw me today, but I was telling them goodbye."

She huffed.

Lorenzo lifted a dark brow at her. "I told them I wouldn't see them anymore and wouldn't meet them ever again. Francesca, I want you. Only you. Do you think it is the same with any other woman? No, it isn't. You think I eat their pussy the way I feast on you?"

She lifted a hand to cover her mouth. Her cheeks flamed at his words. "I don't know. You should have told me. This happened too fast, and I can't just pretend I didn't see you or understand what that means."

"Captain to the bridge," came over the intercom in his cabin.

"*Merda.*" He stalked over to his desk and lifted the receiver on his phone. "What?" he shouted. He stiffened. "Yes, I'll be right there. Get the Coast Guard on the horn and wait for me before you sound the alarm." He hung up the phone and turned to her. "Francesca, we have a medical emergency on board, and I have to go. We will talk later."

He hurried to the ensuite, and she heard the faucet turn on. When he came out, he was buttoning a clean shirt, and his hair was damp. "This takes priority over everything else. I don't know how long until I can leave the bridge."

She nodded. "Yes, I understand."

He hurried out of the cabin, closing the door behind him. Francesca wrapped her arms around herself and gazed out through the sliding door to the balcony. His deep, sexy voice came over the intercom. "Pardon the interruption, ladies and gentlemen. This is Captain DiMarco. We have a medical emergency on board. One of your fellow passengers must be airlifted by the Coast Guard to the nearest hospital. We will be slowing down and preparing. Thank you." As Lorenzo ended the communication, Francesca felt the slight decrease in forward movement as the ship slowed.

She stood in the center of the living room, seeing a side of Lorenzo she didn't realize was there. A man who commanded such a vessel. He commanded all of the crew, and he was responsible for all the guests, even her. Over the past several days, she had almost forgotten he worked all the time.

Francesca, deep in thought, walked out onto the balcony. *The empty movie theater, the intimate dinner in the French restaurant. Although he was constantly working, his crew bent over backwards to please him.*

She looked up when she heard the chop, chop, chop sound of a helicopter. All she saw was a cloudless blue sky. She couldn't see what direction the helicopter came from. A short time later, she could see the helicopter as it turned to go possibly back to Hilo. She hoped whoever they airlifted would be all right.

It was nine o'clock in the evening before Lorenzo came back into the cabin. She turned to see him as he ran his fingers through his hair. He looked tired.

"How are you, Lorenzo?"

"Everything is good. The ship is once again on schedule. Have you eaten?"

"No, I lost track of time."

"Will you eat with me? I want to sit and unwind and most of all, talk to you about Hilo and what you saw."

"Okay." She lifted her chin. "If you're sure. I would like an explanation."

Lorenzo ignored her slight implication as she continued. "I know you had a life before me, but why didn't you tell me when I asked if there was anyone special? So now you say that they weren't." He walked over to the bar and poured himself a whiskey. "Would you like a drink?"

"White wine, thanks." He poured her drink and brought it to her.

"I will tell you everything, but let me order dinner first. What would you like?"

"I'd like a cheeseburger with fries and a Coke. Oh can I have Swiss and grilled mushrooms on the burger, with lettuce, tomato, and a pickle?"

Lorenzo smiled at her. "You found a favorite."

She shrugged a shoulder. "Yes, I love them the best."

He placed the order with his steward and came to sit on the sofa. He toed off his shoes and stretched his legs out before he took a long swig of his drink. "I have to explain why I chose the lifestyle I did. I'm not exactly a swinger. They are generally married or in a relationship with a significant other and like to switch partners. I, on the other hand, wanted no commitment of any kind with anyone. Mindless, free-spirited sex was all I needed… until now."

"I don't understand this. Lorenzo, how come you never came back home to Palermo?"

Ahh, the tough question. He leaned against the back of the sofa, tipping his head and staring at the ceiling. He decided to tell her everything, more than he'd ever told anyone else. Francesca deserved to know.

He lifted his head from the sofa and turned to gaze at her. "The day I left Sicily, my father and I had a huge misunderstanding that led to a terrible argument… There was a young woman I was friends with—only friends—I didn't know she wanted more. Sometimes, the smell of money does crazy things to people. I'm not saying I was a saint. Believe me, I had my share of women, and it was always safe and protected sex. The thing is, she lied and blamed me for her pregnancy. She was having an affair with a married man. I told her I wouldn't marry her. She went to my father with her lies and he believed her.

"He wouldn't listen to me even though I'd never given him cause to mistrust me. My father demanded I marry the girl immediately. I refused and I went to her father. I told him it wasn't me. I never touched her. He said he knew because he overheard his daughter and the man in question agreeing that my father would force me to marry her, and they could continue their affair, while living in the lap of luxury, married to a DiMarco. When I got home, I tried to tell him, but he wouldn't listen. It took the girl's father to convince him." He sighed. "He wouldn't believe me, his own son, over a stranger. I left that day, vowing never to come back. How could I stay? I haven't really talked to my father since."

Lorenzo scrubbed his hand through his hair. "Soon after I left, my father had his first heart attack and Ricardo became

CEO of DiMarco Enterprises. When my father had a second heart attack, Ricardo moved from NYC to Palermo. My brother asked me to join the company as COO of the Contessa Line, but I wouldn't take an executive position and go back to Sicily."

She reached for his hand. "I don't know what to say."

"I had planned on joining the Merchant Marine, then I was accepted to the California Maritime Academy, and that clinched it. I used my own money for my tuition and everything else I needed for the four years. I worked hard and earned every promotion without any special privileges."

After they ate, Lorenzo and Francesca walked out onto the balcony. They heard the distant thrum of music from one of the nightclubs. "Do you miss not going dancing tonight?"

"No, it's nice here with you, Zo. I'm sorry... I have to know. Just tell me, is that the reason for all of the... well... the more than one woman at a time? No commitment to anything?"

"Yes, that's a major part of it, and I'm a true seaman with women in every port."

Her lips turned down at the corners. "Oh, I see. Palermo is a port city."

"Don't do that, Francesca. You are different. Share my bed tonight the way we have these past nights. I promise we will only hold each other. I won't touch you in any way you don't want. This opening up and talking is new to me. I've never told anyone all that I've said to you."

"I'll stay with you, but we have to continue to be open and honest. No more secrets."

He nodded before he handed her one of his t-shirts. "Here, wear this."

She went into his ensuite to change. When she came out, Lorenzo was already in bed, wearing a pair of silk boxers. She climbed into the bed and lay next to him.

"This is all new to you and in a way, me too." He chuckled. "A very new feeling, Imp."

"I'm grateful you understand that I need some time. It was shocking for me… I'm sorry."

"No, Francesca. Don't ever apologize." He brushed a kiss on her temple.

"Tomorrow, when we dock, I would like to take you to Honolulu and spend the day together. A date. Dress casual and wear comfortable shoes. We're going to hike to the top of Diamond Head."

"Okay, that sounds like fun."

He cuddled her close and kissed the top of her head. "*Buona notte*, Francesca."

CHAPTER 10

*I*n the morning Francesca showered and dressed. Putting on a pair of denim cut-off shorts, a white blouse, and her trainers. The ship was slowly gliding into port; she walked out onto the balcony to watch as it came to a stop. His voice came over the ship's communication system. "Ladies and Gentlemen this is Captain DiMarco. Welcome to Honolulu. The authorities have cleared us and we'll begin debarkation shortly. I'll turn the intercom over to our cruise director. He will begin announcing the shore excursions. I hope you all have a wonderful day." Francesca went back into the living room. She grabbed her sunhat and waited for Lorenzo to come back from the bridge.

Lorenzo walked into the cabin. "Good morning, *Tesoro.* I'm free for a few hours. I have to be back around two p.m."

"*Ciao* Zo. Are you going to wear your uniform?" she teased him.

His smile weakened her knees as he said, "Give me a few minutes. There's a backpack on my desk chair. You can put your sunblock in it and anything else you want. Have you eaten?"

"No."

"Good. I want to buy you breakfast once we debark the ship."

"Okay." She grabbed her sketchpad while she waited, working on the dress design she thought of this morning.

Lorenzo walked out of his bedroom. Francesca couldn't stop staring. *He's so handsome and oh so tall.* His cargo shorts accented his narrow waist and muscular legs. The navy-blue t-shirt she bought him yesterday stretched across his chest, barely hiding his abs and his ripped body. The zing of pleasure that zipped through her was a surprise.

Francesca was happy to just be with him. She was thrilled that he chose to be with her and not what he originally planned on doing today—having sex with those two women. He said that in Hilo he didn't do more than take them to lunch to say goodbye.

She believed Lorenzo when he said that he went to tell them that it was over, and he no longer wanted to be involved with them. He'd told her it wasn't really a relationship; it was just sex and fun, nothing other than that. For the two women as well, they wanted the same thing. Never any thought of a relationship or a commitment, just sex. He'd said, 'It's definitely different with you, *tesoro mio.*'

She and Lorenzo rode the officer's elevator down to the debarkation deck. Lorenzo grabbed two bottles of water from a table and slipped them into his backpack, then they turned to the left. "This way to the crew exit." The security guard recognized him and stood at attention.

"At ease," he said. They both handed over their ID to be scanned before they departed the ship. Lorenzo and she walked down the gangway to the pier. There weren't any photographers at this exit.

Francesca's tummy clenched, and she held her breath when she saw two women waiting nearby. *Were they his women in this port?* Yesterday, her brain had been frozen, and she wasn't sure what the women looked like except they were stunning. She vaguely remembered dark hair on both the tall, model-type women. Nothing like her petite form.

One woman hurried over, and Francesca didn't know what to do.

"Oh, Captain DiMarco, thank you so much for helping my father."

Francesca let out the breath she hadn't realized she had held.

The woman continued, "He's so much better. Thank you for insisting that they airlift my mother with him to the hospital. He needed her there, and we've been able to talk with them. Again, thank you for the ship-to-shore line at our disposal."

The other woman said, "Thank you so much, Captain, for everything you've done for my family."

"It was my pleasure to assist. I'm happy that your father is doing well."

Francesca lowered her gaze, confused by her reaction to the women. *What is my problem? Don't I believe him?*

Lorenzo dipped his head close to her, "Are you ready, *Tesoro*?" Taking her hand, he meshed his longer fingers with hers, and they walked down to the end of the pier where a white jeep with its roof and doors removed was parked. "This is our transportation." He helped her into the front seat. "Buckle up, *Tesoro*." Then he walked around to the driver's side and dropped his backpack onto the backseat before climbing in. He turned the ignition and put the jeep in gear.

They drove off, and onto a two-lane palm tree lined road. Traffic at this time of the morning was lite. He stopped in a parking lot not too far from the pier. There were several food trucks parked in a semi-circle. Each offering a different cuisine. The truck's windows were open, and a line of people stood at each waiting to be served. Scattered around the trucks were several tables and chairs, each grouping with their own colorful umbrellas. "I want you to try this. It's called Dole Whip," he said as he held her hand and they walked toward the truck with a sign that read *Hawaii's Specialty*.

Lorenzo ordered two, and they sat, eating the delicious frozen treat. She couldn't help admiring him and how happy she was that he chose to be with her. He'd said in the night, "With you, it's not sex. It's more… it's caring, wanting to know everything about you. We made a connection, more than only a bodily release. You're too young to understand what I mean, Francesca, but I know."

I'm not so innocent. I've been kissed more than a few times. But no one ever made me wet and burn for them or make my breasts ache for their mouth like Zo does.

After breakfast, they drove to Diamond Head. The visitor's center was in the middle of the dormant volcano's crater. He parked and grabbed his backpack from the backseat. Opening it, he said, "You might want to put on more sunblock," handing her the tube.

"Aye, aye, Captain." She saluted him.

Lorenzo lifted his brow, and she couldn't help but giggle. "Is this your first time hiking here?" she asked, taking the tube of sunblock.

"No, but it's my first time with someone, and I'm thrilled that it's you, Imp."

"I feel the same." She applied the sunscreen to her face.

Lorenzo shook his head. "Here, give it to me; you're making a mess." He wiped a big glob from her chin and rubbed it into her face and neck. Francesca stared up into his obsidian eyes. In the black depths a golden fire burned. Her nipples hardened, but she forced herself to ignore her body's reaction to him.

Francesca rubbed some lotion on her arms and down her legs, then handed him the tube. "You have a great tan from being out on the ocean, but you could probably benefit from some."

"Thanks."

She put her hat on, and Lorenzo shoved the tube into his backpack. He purchased the tickets and paid for parking.

Taking her hand, he said, "This way to the trail." He led her through a parklike area with shade trees and benches. "Be warned, it's definitely a hike," he said at the foot of the narrow trail.

A guardrail guided them along a dirt trail. There were signs along the way and photos with QR codes so they could read as they went. They came to a set of steep steps. "You okay?" It was crowded with tourists, some climbing up like them and others on their way down and back to the visitors' center.

"Yes, this is amazing."

"You haven't seen anything yet." He grinned at her. "Come on."

She was grateful for her rock climbing classes and all of the walking up and down hills back home.

After climbing all those steep steps, they reached a tunnel and then more stairs.

"Here, come by this ledge to see the view," he said.

A u-shaped guardrail protected the narrow ledge. Lorenzo stood behind her, his hands resting on her shoulders as they both admired the panoramic view.

"It's beautiful." She twisted to gaze at him. He wore a baseball cap, and his short hair caught the breeze. "Look at the water, such a deep blue." Then she turned, because his lips were too close, and all she wanted to do was feel them on hers.

"Yes, absolutely phenomenal. There's a bunker a bit higher on the ridge," he said.

"I read that this was part of Fort Ruger." She secured her sun hat in the breeze.

They stayed a while longer, enjoying the bird's-eye view of Waikiki sprawled out in the distance and the blue ocean stretching to meet the sky on the horizon.

"Shall we head back, Imp?"

"Okay."

The hike down was faster. They stopped in the gift shop just to browse. She admired a gold Hawaiian bracelet engraved with plumeria flowers before she put it back.

"You did say you were going to feed me lunch before you have to go back to the ship."

"Yes, Imp, but we aren't dressed for anything too fancy. Tonight, we can go for a walk along Waikiki beach and watch the sunset. We can go to dinner after that. I'll have more time. I won't have to be back on the ship until nine. There is a sail-away party that I'm sure you'll enjoy as we leave this port."

"Yes, I'm looking forward to that. The cruise director set up hula lessons on the lido deck and I've been going every day."

"You'll have to demonstrate for me. But right now, what do you say we find a place that serves your new favorite food?"

"Yes, a hamburger! Maybe I'll try a Hawaiian one."

"I have to check-in with the ship. I don't usually stay away for more than an hour or so."

She wouldn't say anything snarky about sex and quickies —well, she wouldn't ruin this time they shared. "I'm sorry if I've kept you from your duties."

"No worries."

Lorenzo twined his fingers with hers as they walked to a food truck. They ordered and found a table to sit at. She fed him a fry, and he licked her fingers. They had a great time eating the burgers and joking. After lunch, they went back to the ship. When they boarded, some of the crew were dressed in fire gear. "What's going on?" Francesca asked.

"They're having a drill."

"Is this normal?"

"Of course. We aren't on vacation. The crew is always working."

"I… I… feel—foolish."

"Don't. How would you know, Imp?" His smile weakened her knees.

They reached the cabin. "I have to change and go to the bridge. Why don't you go to the spa?" He gave her another bone-melting smile. "I arranged for you to have the works. Massage, manicure, pedicure, and anything else you want."

"Yippy." She bounced on her toes and clapped her hands. "I never went to a spa; I'm sure I will love that."

Shaking his head, he said, "Sooo many American expressions." Then he chuckled. "Go, Imp."

She couldn't help herself. She threw her arms around his neck and tugged him to her for a kiss. Something she really wanted to do before she hurried out of the cabin.

THE CRYSTALLINE SPA was on deck nineteen, one deck above the bridge. Francesca stepped off the officer's elevator and walked on to the white marble floor of the reception area. Behind the black granite topped high desk sat two women, both dressed in black spa uniforms. The wonderful fragrance of eucalyptus permeated the air. The first receptionist said,

"Welcome. You must be Ms. Russo. Captain DiMarco asked us to make you comfortable."

"Hello. Yes, you can call me Frankie."

"Okay Frankie, allow me to show you to the changing area. You can leave your belongings there and put on a robe and slippers."

"Thanks."

When she stepped out of her private changing room the other receptionist said, "It will be my pleasure to take you to the massage area." As they walked she saw the spectacular forward view, just like she saw when Lorenzo gave her the tour of the bridge. Although they were docked it was very impressive. "Around this way are more lockers, towels and robes. These are heated tile chaise lounges. Very soothing on the calves, but you are set up for a hot stone massage and then a manicure and pedicure.

"Yes, it will be my first massage."

They walked into a room where ambient music played. The walls were covered in teakwood and the lights were dimmed. In the center was a massage table covered with a white pad. A wonderful scent of lemon and orange wafted throughout. "Hello Miss, I'm Edna and I will be your masseuse."

"Thank you," Francesca's voice was full of excitement as she removed her robe and lay face down on the padded table. Edna's oily fingers kneaded all of the stress from her body. After the steep hike up Diamond Head, this felt wonderful. The relaxing massage ended too soon and Edna escorted her to the Salon. "This is Linda. She will be your manicurist."

"Hello, Miss. Can I offer you something refreshing to drink? We have champagne, mineral water, and flavored water."

"I would love some champagne, thanks."

I'll be right back. In the meantime, please have a seat and choose a color for your toes."

Linda brought her a crystal flute and a china plate with some small bites.

"I hope you don't think I'm rude, but do you really work all the time?" Francesca asked.

"Yes, miss, although we do have some time off. Today, I had about four hours that I was able to go into Honolulu."

"Do you get time off in every port?"

"No, not really, and this is my first time to Hawaii, so I couldn't wait to go sightseeing. I took some pictures to send to my family in Honduras."

"Me too. I did the same to send to my family in Sicily and posted some to my Instagram."

They talked some more and friended each other on social media. Then Francesca went back to the cabin.

Lorenzo walked in. "How do you feel, *Tesoro?*"

"Wonderful, thank you for everything."

"I have something for you." He handed her a jewelry box. "Because you're special to me."

"Zo." She opened the box and saw the solid gold bangle with plumeria flowers that she'd admired earlier. "Thank you."

He took the bracelet from the box. "Allow me to put it on you."

She held out her hand and Lorenzo unclasped the bangle to close over her wrist. "It's so beautiful."

"You're more beautiful… Do you want to change? We can go for our walk on Waikiki Beach, watch the sunset and then have dinner."

"Okay, give me a few minutes."

Francesca changed into a V-neck beach dress with a design of the seashore along the lower third of the mini dress. She gave herself one quick look in the full-length mirror. She smiled, touching the gold bracelet he'd given her before going to the living room.

Lorenzo parked near the restaurant and then they walked along the beach, holding hands. "I'm happy that Stella and I chose Hawaii for a vacay, it's so beautiful."

"It's one of my favorite states. Wait until you see Maui. They have some of the best black sand beaches."

Francesca leaned into him slipping her arm around his waist and he tugged her closer into his side as they walked along the shore. The sun began to set, and Lorenzo stopped walking. "Look out over the water. Maybe we can hear the sun sizzle as the water kisses it." Lorenzo moved to stand behind her as they faced the horizon. He wrapped his arms around her waist, and she leaned against his chest. "You make it sound so beautiful. It's a rare moment to watch *il tramonto*, but you must see the sunset all the time."

"Yes, from the bridge or on deck, but sharing this with you, Francesca, is far better."

"Oh, Zo, you make me feel so special."

He kissed her behind her ear. "I've never enjoyed a day more than I have today with you, *Tesoro*. Tonight, after the party, I hope to make it more special. Something to always remember." She wanted that so much. Lorenzo didn't offer her more of a commitment. She could do this. First, she needed to talk with Stella.

THE CASUAL BEACHSIDE restaurant offered outdoor seating and was perfect after their walk along the white sandy shore. She ordered a lobster roll, which came with seasoned fries. Enough for them to share, and Lorenzo ordered baked oysters for them to share. He ordered crab cakes and lobster bites on the side. They washed everything down with Mai

Tais. The slice of toasted coconut cake was big enough for them to share. Their food server had brought the plate along with two forks.

After Lorenzo paid for dinner they walked from the restaurant to the parking lot.

"Zo, I want to call Stella and see how she's doing. As long as I'm not near the ship, I can use my phone and not get charged all of the added fees. You go back to the ship and after I call her, I'll find my way back."

"Come back to the cabin and use my code. I have my own personal plan with unlimited minutes."

She hesitated. "Okay. If you're sure, I'll call her when we get back on board."

"You will have privacy. I'll be on the bridge. You can even video chat if you want."

"Oh, yes. I would like that very much. I'd get to see her, thank you."

Once they returned to the ship, Lorenzo showered and changed into his uniform. Francesca couldn't wait to talk with her friend. She sat cross-legged on her bed in her bedroom. Using Lorenzo's code, she dialed Stella's number.

"Hi, how are you feeling? I hope it's not too early to call you."

Stella sat up in her bed. She smoothed her chestnut curls and smiled. "No, I'm just resting. See, I'm dressed. I can't believe we're video chatting. I'm walking with only one crutch, and I see the doctor again next week. My physical therapist is happy with my progress. By the time you return from vacation, I should be back on track for our boutique."

"Oh Stella, that's the best news. You do look good."

"You look fabulous and have a nice tan going on. Tell me, how is the cruise?"

"The cruise is great, but I need your advice."

"What is it? Tell me."

Francesca told her about the group of swingers. Everything except Lorenzo's preference to have sex with more than one woman at a time. She didn't want to lie to Stella about any of that, but it was Lorenzo's business and not her business to tell. Not even to her BFF.

"When we walked off the ship, I saw… a…woman waiting. I got nervous thinking it was his *date*—"

"Was it?"

"No."

Stella tipped her head to one side and furrowed her brow. "Do you trust him?"

"I want to." She searched for her true feelings before she answered her friend. "Yes, I do trust Lorenzo."

"If he told you, then he wants to be with you. You believe him, right? Trust is the basis for any relationship. Without that, you have nothing no matter how good the sex is." Her friend leaned forward. "So, was your first time all you wanted it to be?"

Francesca's lips curved into a huge smile. "Mmm, yes, and so much more. No words could describe his gentleness. I never knew."

They laughed about the condom and her not understanding why he left the bed. Then they talked about her ex.

Stella said, "You told me that his kisses did nothing for you. You worried if that was all there was, then why bother. Now, with Lorenzo—"

"He ignited a fire in me. I crave his touch… I never understood that before him."

"I hope one day to feel the same as you do. Show me the cabin."

Francesca walked around her room and then out to the living room and finally to the balcony with the pool.

"OMG, it's beautiful."

"Better than our cabin on Deck 3. It was lonely down

there for two reasons: one, you weren't there, and two, there was no porthole. It was always dark. Next time, no inside cabin. They did have a screen that mimicked the outside, but what am I, in a movie?"

She panned her phone around so Stella could get a view of the water, then she sat out on one of the cushioned chairs. "That first day with the jet lag, I never knew what time it was." She giggled. "I woke up at three a.m. thinking it was breakfast time. I dressed before I looked at the time, then I thought it was afternoon."

"That must have been funny. Too bad I missed it."

"Yes, now it is but then, I wasn't laughing. If you were here you would have your phone set with all the wake up reminders."

Lorenzo's voice came over the loudspeaker. "That's him," Francesca whispered.

"Good evening, ladies and gentlemen. I hope you enjoyed our time in Honolulu. We're waiting for one more excursion to arrive, and then we will set sail in approximately thirty minutes. Enjoy the sail-away party on the lido deck. The bar is open, and drinks are on me until we depart."

"He sounds sexy." Stella held up her iPad. "I'm looking at his picture. Very handsome."

"Yes, he is."

"After your ex, you deserve a man. One who treats you right."

"I can't believe how wonderful he is. Your cousins were right about how great it is with the right person. I'm happy I waited."

"Also, Francesca, Lorenzo is older and a real man. You know what I mean. Some people frown on the age-gap thing, but I think if you're mature, then it's a good thing. And you are definitely mature and know what you want."

"Thank you."

Talking with Stella always put things in the proper perspective. Francesca would see where this thing with Zo would go. When she ended the call with Stella, she changed into a Hawaiian print dress and went to the lido deck. Although they weren't sailing yet, the party was already in full swing. She found some of her tablemates, and they talked about their day in Honolulu, enjoying the free drinks. Then they all joined in and danced the hula. Francesca and her friends had met every morning on the lido deck to learn the steps to the hula.

After the party, she went back to the cabin, thinking about Zo and what would happen after the cruise. There was no talk about that or when she went home. Would they keep in touch? Would he go back to his lifestyle? Forget her? What did she want? There were too many questions without answers. She couldn't make any decisions now. She had too many piña coladas at the sail-away party. What she wanted now was for Zo to make love to her. He'd said he would be free and return to the cabin two hours after departure.

CHAPTER 11

Lorenzo walked into his cabin, and the first thing he noticed was Francesca, in a seductive dress, reclining on the sofa. "I've been waiting for you."

Her sexy whisper excited him more than seeing her naked. He unbuttoned his uniform shirt as he closed the distance between them. *I want her with me all the time.* He sat on the edge of the couch, his hip snug into the curve of her waist. He rested one hand on the back of the sofa and bent to her. "You have?"

Francesca slid her warm hand over his bare chest, stopping to rub her fingers into his mat of black hair. "Kiss me, Zo."

He brushed his lips over hers. She moved her hands to touch his cheeks with the tips of her fingers. "It's not fair." She pouted. "Your eyelashes are longer than mine." She giggled.

"Did you enjoy the sail-away party?"

"Yes." Then she whispered in his ear, "I may have had a little too much to drink."

He turned and nipped her earlobe. "I know."

"Take me to bed." Lorenzo lifted her from the couch, and Francesca hooked her silky arms around his neck before she tugged his head to her. She kissed him, a kiss that had him debating if he should take her in this slightly inebriated state. Lorenzo carried her to his bed. Laying her down, he slipped her sandals from her feet, then covered her with the blanket.

"Zo, what are you doing?"

"Putting you to bed. I'll join you soon."

"Okay," she sighed.

He watched as her smile spread and her eyes closed.

She was such an imp. He went into the living room, poured himself a whiskey, and walked out onto the balcony. He loved the salty ocean breeze on his face and the scent of the briny Pacific Ocean. He was content to have Francesca here in his bed. He finished his drink and walked into his bedroom. Lorenzo undressed and, taking her in his arms, he fell asleep. Sometime during the night, Francesca rolled on top of him. "Zo, are you awake?"

"Now I am." He ran his hand along her body.

"Why am I still dressed?" She pushed up on his chest. "But you're naked. Did I fall asleep?"

"Yes."

"I'm sorry."

"Don't be," he said as he flipped her onto her back. Piece by piece, her dress fell away, then her bra and panties, revealing her seductive body to him. "Francesca, I need you." He kissed her lips as her hands skimmed over his body. He sucked one of her pink nipples into his mouth, teasing it into a hard peak with his tongue before he moved to the other.

Her hands traveled over his back, and she moaned, "Zo, please."

He lifted his head from her breasts and, taking her with him, he sat up against the headboard. He reached for the condom, ripped the packet open, and rolled it on. "Wow. I have no words."

He grinned at her before he lifted her over him. "Spread your knees over my hips." She did, and he saw the uncertainty in the blue depths of her eyes.

He held his erection. "Now take me into your hot pussy."

Her blond hair falling over her shoulders, a blush spread across her cheeks. He knew that Francesca was shy about his sex talk. She looked down at where he held his erection, then she lifted her gaze to him. "Like this?" she said, moving to take the tip of his cock into her.

"Yes, lower yourself all the way down on my dick."

"Oh, Zo this is… ahh."

"Yes, Imp, you ride me. Set the pace." As he spoke, he touched her clit, pressing the excited bud as she rose and lowered herself on him. "Do you like that?"

"*Si, si*, ahhh, just like that."

He snaked his other arm around her, pulling her head down to capture her lips. Lorenzo nipped at her bottom lip before he thrust his tongue into her waiting mouth. Her breath caught in little moans before Francesca shrieked with her pleasure as her core clutched and caressed him. Lorenzo slipped his finger over her wet clit as Francesca shattered in his arms, screaming his name.

This is all he ever wanted to hear, his name on her kiss-swollen lips as she surrendered to the pleasure he gave her. Her hot pussy contracted around him before she fell against him, panting his name. When she calmed, he cradled her in his arms. She touched his cheek. "What about you?"

"Oh, you thought we're finished? Believe me, we are far from that."

She giggled. "That's good. I want more."

Lorenzo turned her in his arms… kissing her, loving her. Once they were satisfied, he held her lethal body in his arms, his fingers sliding through her lustrous blond hair. "Tomorrow, we will be in Maui, and we're invited to Giorgio and Madeline's house. My brother will be there, and I'm sure he wants to convince me to go back to Palermo and be the COO of the Contessa Line. Work at a desk and be away from what I love, the sea. This isn't what I want. All those years ago, my father didn't listen to me when I said that I had never touched that girl. He said I dishonored the family name and how disappointing I was to him. Now, my brother isn't listening. I won't take a desk job."

Francesca kissed his neck, her fingers sliding through his chest hairs. "I understand how you feel… But I'm sad because that leaves us nowhere." She lifted her head and gazed into his eyes. "I'm sorry… I shouldn't have said that to you. It looks as if I'm not listening to you either."

He snuggled her into the circle of his arms. "*Tesoro*, I know we have a lot to work out. Let's try to sleep. Tomorrow will be a busy day."

The next morning, he woke her with kisses down her body. "Mmmm, that feels so nice."

He spread kisses over her abdomen. "We are about two hours from dropping anchor." He nudged her legs apart and nuzzled the inside of first one thigh, then the other. Lorenzo's morning stubble excited her then his fingers stroked over her before his tongue teased her seam open. Lorenzo wedged his shoulders between her legs. She loved what he did with his tongue, driving her to the brink of orgasm more than once. Stopping and starting again, but never touching her clit. He traced her folds with his tongue, teasing her, not thrusting into her or touching her clit.

"Zo, Zo…please," she panted. She needed his masterful tongue on her clit. Francesca spread her legs wider, pushing herself against his mouth. "Please… make me come."

He sucked her clit.

"Yes. Yes, *Dio mio.*" Her fingers tangled in his hair, then her thighs clenched his head. He slid a finger deep into her and curled the tip over her g-spot. Her entire body shuddered. Every nerve ending in her body quivered.

Her orgasm crested like an ocean wave. She tilted her head back as ecstasy took over. Lorenzo turned her into a madwoman. She was covered in a fine mist. Short gasps of pleasure escaped her and his tongue kept her on the brink of another orgasm. He stroked her g-spot again, and she thrashed and moaned as the waves of a second orgasm washed over her.

Lorenzo crawled up her sated body. "You're beautiful."

She touched his lips with her finger.

He brushed his lips over hers, kissing her slowly before he lifted her from the bed. He walked over to the wall and moved his arm from under her knees. She stood, her back against the wall. "Zo?"

"I have to be in your hot pussy now."

"Yes," she shrieked.

He moved from her long enough to grab a condom from the nightstand. Once he rolled on the protection, he lifted her, and she wrapped her legs around him. She moaned his name. Looping her arms around his neck, he pressed her against the wall, his big hands holding her buttocks as he thrust into her.

"Oh, Zo, you feel so good."

He kissed her neck, moving to suck a nipple into his mouth. She arched her back, pushing her breasts into the mat of hair on his chest. He lifted and lowered her onto his enormous erection. Tension coiled inside her, and she loved what he did. Pleasure sizzled through her body with each of his powerful thrusts. Another orgasm gripped her.

"Yes, *Tesoro*, I feel your pussy coming around my cock." He groaned, thrusting once more into her. Lorenzo threw his head back. The cords of muscles in his neck and shoulders stood out as he gnashed his teeth. She felt his explosion in her core, setting off another set of contractions. He held her to the wall while he kissed her neck. His hot breath panting. *I love him. I love him more than I thought possible to love another person. I'm in deep trouble!*

"We have time for a quick shower before we drop anchor."

"I don't know if I can move."

She felt his gentle kiss on her brow. His lips stayed as he said, "No worries, I will carry you. It will be my pleasure to wash you."

After the shower, Lorenzo said, "I have to go to the bridge. This is a tender port, so the guests will be ferried to shore by the *Diamond of the Seas'* own boats. Once we receive clearance, I'll come back to change, and we can go."

"Okay, that sounds good. I'll order breakfast and get dressed."

Once he left, Francesca ordered coffee and two pastries for them. Then she tied her hair up in a ponytail, put on makeup and a yellow sundress that she had made for the vacation. She walked out to the balcony, breathed in the fresh air, and gazed at the lush island of Maui. She sat reading her book while waiting for Lorenzo.

He walked out onto the balcony. "You look stunning, *Tesoro.* I won't be too long."

Francesca poured his espresso into a cup and handed it to him. He drank the coffee in one gulp before he went to change. A short time later, he came out of the bedroom in a pale-blue silk shirt, open at the collar, his sleeves rolled up to his elbows. He wore navy slacks. "Did you pack a bathing suit?"

"Yes, I did."

"Good, then let's go."

He meshed his fingers with hers, and they took the elevator down to the debarkation deck. They walked to the crew side where a tender waited to take them to shore.

At the dock, he found their car. "Giorgio left his Lamborghini for us to use."

"I've never ridden in such an amazing car."

He snickered. "My cousin and both my brothers love their Lamborghinis."

"What do you drive? Well… besides, driving me crazy."

His lips curved up, revealing white-even-teeth in a dazzling smile. "Ha, ha, Imp, it's the other way around. You drive me crazy, but to answer your question, I drive a Maserati."

She laughed. "Of course you do. Its logo is a Triton."

"Before we go to my cousin's, there is a place I want to show you. The black sand beach here is one of the most beautiful."

Lorenzo turned the Lamborghini down a narrow two-lane road with wild tropical foliage on both sides. The road made a sharp bend and after that, on one side was a paved parking lot and on the other a dirt road. He drove down the dirt road. "You should get your camera ready, *Tesoro*."

"It's already so beautiful. I can't imagine more."

"Wait, you'll see."

The road ended in a cove, just before the ocean. Francesca gasped. Lorenzo parked the Lamborghini next to two other cars. Spread out before them a carpet of black sand, the white foam of the ocean waves kissed the black beach and the blue water of the Pacific spread out, almost touching the cloudless blue sky above.

Francesca slipped her sandals off and jumped out of the car. Snapping photos, she turned to him. "Zo, let's take a selfie."

He removed his shoes and rolled up his pants legs.

Lorenzo bent down to Francesca and placed his arm around her shoulders. She snapped the photo.

"Here, look at us." She showed him her phone screen. "Don't we look cute with the beach behind us?"

"Yes, *tesoro*." Then he rested his chin on her shoulder and she made bunny ears on his head with one hand and snapped the photo with the other. She giggled. "I'm posting this one on Instagram."

"No. Not that one." He laughed, his arms around her waist as he nipped at her neck. She snapped another photo of them. Then he lifted her in his arms and walked to the water's edge. Lorenzo spun her around.

Her arms tightened around his neck. "You better not drop me. I didn't bring a change of clothes."

"I won't." He snuggled her high up on his broad chest. "We had better go, so we aren't late."

Not too far from the parking area there was a shower-head with a knob. Lower on the pipe, a faucet jutted out that was perfect to rinse your feet. Lorenzo opened the front hood of the Lamborghini and removed two towels. They dried their feet and then Lorenzo rolled his pants down and put his shoes on.

Francesca slipped into the front seat, and Lorenzo closed her door for her. She admired the beach one last time. Then he turned on the ignition and drove back to the main highway.

Francesca sat in the car, scrolling through her photos. "Zo I can't believe how absolutely beautiful Hawaii is."

"We're almost there."

He seemed to tense as he drove. "What's wrong, Zo?"

He didn't take his eyes off the road. "Nothing. What could possibly be wrong? I didn't tell you, but before we left the ship, my brother texted me, reminding me why he's here."

"Wouldn't this be the logical next step for you?"

"Not for me. I won't be forced to go back to Sicily. I told him I won't. My home is my ship and my condo in San Diego."

"I get it." *This is his way of telling me that all we had was a fling which will end when the cruise ends.* The lump in her stomach traveled to her throat.

"Here we are." Lorenzo parked in the driveway of an elegant two-story contemporary home that fit perfectly with the landscape of the island. He opened her door, and she stepped out of the car. Lorenzo kissed her hand, before meshing his longer fingers with hers. They walked up the lush, tropical, landscaped stone path to the main house. The front of the home faced a private, white, sandy beach.

Lorenzo rang the doorbell. Giorgio opened the door. He was just as tall as Lorenzo, with the same jet black hair, but where Lorenzo had black eyes, Giorgio had Aqua eyes.

"Hey cuz," he said before he turned to her. "Francesca, it's good to see you after all these years. This is my wife Madeline."

The woman standing next to Giorgio was stunning, with long blond beach wave hair and moss green eyes. "*Benvenuta Francesca,*" she said in perfect Italian.

"Thank you and a pleasure to meet you," Francesca replied in Italian.

Giorgio wore a very Hawaiian shirt with shorts. He switched to English, gesturing at Lorenzo he said, "Why so formal, cousin? The firing squad won't be called upon today." He chuckled. "Rico is in the living room with Liz."

"With my brother here, you never know," Lorenzo snarked.

Giorgio patted him on the back. "This way."

The main living area opened onto an infinity pool and spa. The stacking sliding doors were open, making the indoor-outdoor space flow effortlessly from one to the other. Palm trees and lush tropical foliage surrounded the house and then past the strip of sand, the blue of the ocean met the cloudless blue sky. The sound of the waves breaking onto the shore was relaxing.

Liz looked beautiful in a white sundress with her red hair flowing around her shoulders. She was five months pregnant, and Ricardo doted on her. She teased him, saying it was bordering on stalking the way he hovered over her.

Ricardo was slightly taller than Lorenzo, but he had the same black hair and pitch black eyes. Francesca couldn't miss the family resemblance.

Ricardo placed his hand on his wife's belly. "I missed your first pregnancy, and I don't want to be deprived of one moment of this one."

"Yes, well, that's in the past and better left there."

Lorenzo said, "Speaking of which, how is your mother, Giorgio?"

Giorgio narrowed his eyes. "You know very well how she is. Married to Andre and pregnant with twins. Hopefully, he can prevent her from causing more trouble."

Francesca had no idea what they were talking about, but she knew Lorenzo was purposefully provoking his older brother. When she had a moment alone with him, she said, "Is it wise to play with fire?" He dragged her into him.

"Only your kind of fire do I want to play with." He kissed her neck. "The heat of your pussy when I sink into you."

"Zo!"

"Yes, *Tesoro*. Maybe we can find a private spot, and I can show you."

"Stop teasing. What happened?"

He kissed the tip of her nose. "I never joke about making love with you. If you insist… I can tell you what I know. Liz and Ricardo were dating, and their relationship had progressed, becoming very serious, with promises of marriage, when somehow… There is much that we don't know, but my Aunt Angela, Giorgio's mother, was behind the breakup of my brother and Liz. Aunt Angela weaved lies and deception. While they were apart, Liz had Ricardo's son, and he didn't know anything about that until one day just before Christmas last year, Rico and my sister-in-law Sofia had gone Christmas shopping. They walked into Cartier on Fifth Avenue, where Liz worked. He saw her, and then he found out he had a son. Knowing my brother, Liz had no choice but to marry him and move to Palermo. His son Tony is almost four and to see him, he looks exactly like Rico."

"What about your aunt?" Francesca asked. "I've met her on occasion and she's always in mourning black. Now you say she's having twins. Isn't Giorgio… like thirty-four?"

"Yes. There's more to that tangled web of deceit I don't know, but she manipulated Andre Bourbon, Giorgio's friend, to help separate Liz and Rico. Andre didn't know the extent of his involvement. He bought stocks in the company for Angela, so she could take over the company." He grit his teeth. "Manipulative Sicilian women."

"Oh yes, it's a family-owned business, and you're part of it with your own billions of dollars. That's why your brother is fighting so hard for you to take your rightful place."

"That's beside the point. I have my reasons. One day I will do what they want, but for now… I can't."

The three couples sat around a patio table on the lanai overlooking the crystal-clear water, while Madeline's housekeeper served a formal lunch. *Pranzo* in Italy was a big midday meal and that is exactly what was served. They began with *Pasta alla Norma* a fried eggplant and fresh tomato and basil served over homemade pasta. That was followed by roasted pork with baby potatoes and a green bean salad. Wine from Giorgio's private stock was served with every course. Everyone but Liz drank the wine. The meal ended with Sicilian pastries. Cannoli and assorted cookies including Francesca's favorite, pine nut cookies.

Liz and Madeline were friendly and when they asked, Francesca told them about the boutique she and Stella were opening.

Lorenzo put his arm around Francesca's shoulder. "You should see her designs. Francesca, isn't what you're wearing one of your creations?"

"Yes, Zo, it is."

Liz said, "I would love to see your sketches."

"Yes, Francesca, me too."

She scrolled through her phone and found some of her favorites to show them. Francesca promised to invite them to the grand opening. Madeline said, "I met your brother Gus and your sister-in-law Sara when Giorgio took me to Erice. They have a fabulous restaurant."

"I help them out from time to time. I must have been in Palermo when you were there. I'm going to open the boutique in Palermo, near my parents and my business partner, Stella. She doesn't want to leave her family either, so Palermo is the perfect choice."

While the housekeeper cleared the table. Madeline said, "Liz, Francesca, would you like to go for a walk on the beach to help us digest?"

"Oh, yes. Let me get my sun hat out of my bag," Francesca said.

"I'll be right back. I have to change my shoes and grab my hat as well."

"Okay, I'll meet you out back," Madeline said.

"While you ladies go for a walk, Rico, Lorenzo, and I are going to the study. We have some matters to discuss," Giorgio said.

The three men excused themselves and walked into the study. Ricardo sat on a deep blue over stuffed sofa while

Giorgio slid an arm chair closer for Lorenzo. Then Giorgio took a seat opposite Ricardo.

Ricardo said, "I know Dad can be stubborn, and you have the same tendency, but hasn't this gone on long enough? Ten years, man. We all know what happened with that girl."

"Then you should understand how strongly I feel. He never even asked me if it was true. If the child she carried was mine. He believed her lies *and* her tears." Lorenzo slammed his fist against his thigh before he stood. "Telling me that I would marry her that very day. He didn't believe me when I told him I'd never touched her. He wouldn't listen. I don't want to talk to him or be in the same city as him. If it weren't for the girl's father, I would have been married to someone who lied and would cuckold me."

Giorgio nodded. "Come on, sit down. We all have overbearing parents, but your dad doesn't run the company anymore. Rico is CEO. You know this and that we started the Contessa Line, with you in mind. The plan was always for you to take over the operations. Look at all your accomplishments. The youngest sea captain in the world, and there is no nepotism in that. You've earned every promotion, and this is the next logical step."

"I don't want to come home to Palermo. I vowed never to be in the same city as him, or the same country for that matter. I want to stay as captain of the *Diamond of the Seas*."

"The line is growing, and we need you to take charge. You know that the corporate headquarters are in Palermo. We can't ask all the staff to move for you, or would you rather we let them go and hire new people for you in San Diego or Miami? Why are you so pigheaded?" Ricardo ran his fingers through his hair. "Dad isn't involved. One of these days, you will have to sit down and talk to him. Mom keeps quiet about all of this, but it's really hurting her—"

"I spoke with Mom, and I saw her a few weeks ago in Cabo San Lucas when she came for a visit."

"You need to come back home."

Lorenzo jumped out of his seat and cut the air before him with his hand in an angry gesture. "*No, basta non vengo.* Enough, I'm not coming back." He strode to the door.

The women had returned from their walk along the beach and Francesca heard the shouting, recognizing Lorenzo's voice. "I will not be forced. I will hand in my resignation before I come back."

Liz and Madeline heard it as well. Liz said, "Sometimes, the DiMarco men need time to realize what is right."

Lorenzo stormed into of the room. "Francesca, it's time to go. Liz, take care of yourself. Your husband can be a mule at times." He bent and kissed her before he turned to Madeline. "A pleasure as always to see my favorite cousin-in-law." He kissed her on both cheeks, then Francesca said goodbye to the two women.

Giorgio smacked Lorenzo on his back. "Take care of yourself." Then he whispered loud enough for all to hear, "We all have relatives that we have to humor."

Ricardo blustered, "Humor, is that—"

Liz put her hand on her husband's chest. "Darling, we're here for a pleasant visit and not to make Francesca uncomfortable." Ricardo covered his wife's hand with his before he bent to kiss her temple. "*Si, amore.*"

Madeline held Francesca's hands. "Giorgio and I won't be home until next month. I'll call you. Maybe you can come over for *pranzo.*"

"Thank you. I would like that." She kissed both women and hugged both men before she and Lorenzo drove back to the ship. Once they were on the road, he called to get an update on the ship and to have a tender waiting to take them back to the *Diamond of the Seas*.

Lorenzo visibly calmed as he drove back to the dock. He talked to Francesca about his responsibilities and his need to do as his brother asked. Now, they were calling on him to step up, and he wasn't ready to give up his freedom and take on the added responsibility.

CHAPTER 12

When they entered the captain's cabin, Lorenzo pulled Francesca into his arms. "You kept me strong today. I'm happy that you were with me." He brushed a stray curl from her face. "Did you have a good time with Liz and Madeline?"

"Yes, they're very nice."

He buried his face in her neck, smelling her scent before he kissed her neck, nipping at the delicate flesh of her earlobe. "I've missed you all day."

"Me too, Zo." She reached up, looping her arms around his neck as she rose on her toes. He kissed her lips, at first with feather-light sweeps, before he parted them with his.

Francesca responded with her own set of demands, her tongue sparring with his. Lorenzo bent, slipping his arm under her knees. He lifted her soft seductive curves into his arms and carried her into his bedroom.

"I need you so much, *tesoro*." He toed off his shoes. Then he kissed her again.

"Yes, Zo, me too," she mumbled against his lips before she lifted her fingers to his cheeks and ravaged his mouth.

Gradually her hands slid down his chest and Francesca worked at the buttons of his silk shirt as he laid her in the center of his bed. Following her down, he covered her with his strong body before he straddled her. He lifted the hem of her yellow sundress. "Sit up so I don't rip the dress."

"You can."

"No, it's too pretty to damage."

She lifted her arms over her head, and he pulled the dress from her. It silently glided to the floor. He unhooked her cream-colored lace bra. Lorenzo sat back, keeping his weight off her legs as he admired her. "I can't get enough of you. I could make love to you all day and all night," he said working the rest of the buttons of his shirt before tossing it to the floor. His Gucci leather belt followed silently landing on top if his silk shirt.

Francesca ran her small hands over his torso, burying her fingers in his chest hairs. She sat up and kissed his neck, his chest, before her nails teased him as her fingers slid over every muscle of his abdomen. "You feel so good. Marble-hard washboard abs."

"Something else is hard and ready for you," he growled in a low, husky voice.

She giggled. "Oh yes," she said, running her hand over his crotch. Then she lay back against the pillows.

He crouched over her, and she lifted her hips to shimmy out of her panties. She stroked his cheek with her fingers. "This is where I always want to be. Naked and in your arms. When you hold me like this, the world goes away, and it's just the two of us." She moistened her lips with her tongue.

He unzipped his fly. "*Tesoro*, I know I'm asking you to give up so much for me. I love you, and I want us to be together."

"Zo, I love you too and want to be with you. Why can't you give Palermo a chance? Try to see my side of this."

His brow furrowed, and his lips pressed together in a

grim line. Her words worked better than a cold shower ever could. *I knew better than to believe in love. All women lie to get what they want. Look at my aunt, the girl in Italy. Now Francesca. It's better to let her down easily right now.* Shaking his head. "No. *Tesoro,* you have your whole life before you. Someday, you will meet—"

She pushed at him, and he moved off her. "Someday what?" she said as she swept her blond hair from her beautiful face. "I'll meet someone who will love me and want to live where I am. Give me all my dreams, but it isn't you. Is that what you were going to say, Lorenzo? I'll get married one day. I'll be in someone else's arms. He'll see my body the way you see it now. Is that what you want? You said I was the only one. Were they empty words? There will be no one but you for me. I guess that's not how you feel. You'll go back to whatever it is you do with your women. I couldn't possibly—"

"What has gotten into you?" He grabbed her shoulders and slammed his lips on hers. A demanding kiss.

An angry flush covered her cheeks. She pulled her mouth from his. "It's over. I want to go back to my cabin on Deck 3."

He threw his head back as if she'd slapped him. "No," his voice thundered out of him. "You think your cabin was lonely? Would you like to see the brig?"

"What?" Her eyes rounded in surprise.

All he did was arch a brow.

"You wouldn't dare. I won't let you."

"Then be reasonable, Francesca."

"I am. I've made up my mind. When this cruise ends, I'm going home."

"That's it then? You've decided."

"Yes." She shoved him and leapt from the bed. Grabbed her clothes from the floor and stormed past him in a naked huff.

The slamming of his bedroom door reverberated through him. Lorenzo took a deep breath and slowly let it out. The emptiness of his bedroom without Francesca already overwhelmed him. It was as empty as his life. "Women," he muttered, zipping his slacks and walking barefoot from his bedroom to the bar. He poured himself a whiskey. They would be in Maui for another four hours. He called the head of security. "This is Captain DiMarco. I want to know if Miss Francesca Russo debarks the ship."

"Do you want her detained, Captain?"

"No. Let me know. Understand?" Lorenzo slammed the phone down on its cradle and walked out onto the balcony.

She doesn't love me—I chose this life and uncommitted sex for this very reason. It's what I want. No closeness. I'm a fool to think any different. This is what I want.

FRANCESCA HAD GONE BACK to her bedroom. She dressed in shorts and a top before she flounced down on her bed. *How dare he threaten me.* Taking in some calming breaths, she decided to go find some of her friends. When the elevator arrived, she pressed the button for the promenade deck.

She walked out onto the open deck. There were a few passengers walking around, while some sat under open umbrellas, enjoying the view of Maui in the distance. The ship's tenders were going to and from the island. She couldn't find any of her friends, so she went and got a gelato. Sitting in the shade looking out at the blue water, a plane flying overhead, she couldn't stop herself from thinking of Lorenzo. She loved him, of that she was positive, but she couldn't stay with him. *Why can't he understand how I feel?* She finished her gelato and was almost tempted to get another one, instead she went back to sit in the shade choosing to stay out of his cabin.

"Ladies and gentlemen, this is Captain DiMarco. I hope you enjoyed Maui. I was just informed that all the passengers were back on board, and we'll be departing for our next port in ten minutes. Thank you and have a pleasant evening."

Francesca went back to his cabin and into her room to dress for dinner. On her pillow in a fluted foil cup was a strawberry-shaped marzipan piece of candy. The almond confection was her favorite, and on her nightstand, a velvety soft gardenia in a bud vase. She ate the candy, savoring the flavor, and sniffed the wonderful fragrant flower. Then she changed into a short dress and put on her heels. She placed her key to his cabin, a tube of lipstick, and her ship ID into the tiny silver crossbody purse. She left her phone in her room, not in the mood to take any pictures.

Francesca walked out of the cabin and took the elevator down two decks. She went to sit in one of the many lounges around the ship. She ordered a glass of white wine and listened to the music.

"Hi Frankie, are you coming to the dining room tonight?" Claire asked as she sat down on the couch opposite her.

"Yes. I was going to see what your plans are."

"Tonight, we were going to skip the show and go dancing. Have an early night because tomorrow we all signed up to go surfing."

"I had wanted to do that."

"Come with us. The shore excursion desk is open. Let's see if you can purchase the same tour, so we can all go together."

"Okay."

They walked to the desk, and Francesca bought the ticket. Then the dinner chimes sounded that the main dining room was open, and it was time for dinner. The maître d' welcomed them and they went to their table. Francesca pushed her food around her plate, trying to keep her sadness to herself. Her tablemates at least kept her mind off of Lorenzo talking about dancing and tomorrow's surfing excursion.

❧

THEIR LAST PORT in Hawaii could have been fun if she didn't spend her time thinking of Lorenzo. Surfing was definitely an adventure. Their group had a two-hour lesson before they could try their hand at surfing. Francesca realized she needed more than that amount of time to get the hang of this. Her instructor was cute and flirted with her, but she pretended to not understand.

While the group had lunch on the beach, she laughed and joked. They'd passed around their phones with the photos they took.

"Frankie, look at this." It was a photo of her in her yellow polka-dot bikini, the surf leash around her ankle. She was crouching down on a blue-and-white-stripe board just before she lost her balance and fell into the water. She swiped to the next photo, and there she was in the water.

She laughed. "Great shot. Can you send them to me?"

"Sure thing."

Once lunch was over, some of her shipmates went back in the water while others walked along the beach. Francesca decided it was the perfect time to call Stella. She wanted to find out how her friend's doctor appointment went. "Hi, I had a minute and wanted to talk to you. How was your follow-up visit?"

"Everything is wonderful, and my surgeon is happy with my progress. The incision is healing nicely, and I'm doing great. How are you?"

"I guess I'm okay. I can't wait to get home."

"Really? What happened with you and Lorenzo? Last time we talked, you were trying to hold back the days."

"How did you know it's him?"

"This is me, Stella, your BFF. Remember?"

Francesca laughed at that. "Well, he's being a jerk and isn't thinking of my feelings. He has an opportunity to move back to Palermo, and he won't do it. Not even to be near me. He practically told me that he wanted me to meet someone else."

"Are you kidding? He said that to you?"

"Pretty much… I think… he'd rather I stay with him, but we have our plans, and I don't want to renege on that."

"Well, the DiMarcos are a powerful and rich family. They're all billionaires, even Lorenzo. If a billionaire asked me to stay with him, I would."

"You know that his money doesn't interest me. Not even his very prestigious last name."

"Okay, I guess you have a lot to think about, but as far as our business, we can always adapt to whatever will work for us. You don't have to be here in Palermo all the time."

"I'm so glad I got to talk to you. You always put things in perspective for me. Oh, I have to go. My group is calling me."

"Take care and have fun."

"Thanks."

She spent more time with Claire and her tablemates and less time in the cabin, avoiding Lorenzo as much as possible. In the morning, she showered and dress. Then she went to have breakfast in the dining room with her friends. At night, she found another marzipan candy on her pillow and a fresh fragrant gardenia on the nightstand.

She and her friends went to karaoke on the second at sea night. *Were there only sad breakup songs in the mix?* She had to get out of the lounge. Francesca waved bye to her friends and went back to his cabin. She found Lorenzo in her bedroom. "You've been doing this? I thought it was Mario."

He lifted a black brow at her. "Why would my steward leave you candy and flowers, Imp?"

Her chin lifted. "My mistake."

"Why are you acting like this?"

Francesca couldn't miss the frustration in his deep voice. She shrugged a shoulder. "Why are you acting like an overgrown child? I may be twelve years younger than you and not very worldly, but in this, I'm much more mature. Yes, what your father did, not trusting you or listening to you was wrong but now, your behavior doesn't make it right or any better."

He didn't answer her. Lorenzo turned and walked out of her room.

Oh, he could be infuriating. Even with his jaw set in a stubborn line, that five o'clock shadow and his sensuous lips pressed into a thin line, he was so handsome. He made her knees weak. She ached for him. Just the two of them sharing a cocktail and talking about their day. How they'd opened up to each other. Talking about their past.

CHAPTER 13

*L*orenzo sat in his captain's chair on the bridge. The blue of the Pacific stretching before him. The ocean was calm just small ripples without any white caps. A few seagulls flapped their wings, soaring over the ship. One dove into the water and then flew up to join the other gulls.

Lorenzo chatted with his chief engineer for a while, laughing at a joke he told. There was normal activity on the bridge, nothing unusual. His thoughts wandered. Tonight, was the last formal night before the cruise ended. A ball would be held in the grand ballroom. Would Francesca be there?

He hadn't seen her since she caught him putting the marzipan candy on her pillow. *I miss her. No.* He clenched his fist. *My feelings are under my control.* That night, in her bedroom, he'd turned and walked out before he grabbed her and satisfied his need on her lustrous body. Making her accept what they have. He'd never had to force a woman, and he wouldn't dare hurt Francesca.

"Two whales on the port side, Captain." The officer of the watch held his binoculars to his eyes.

Lorenzo leaned forward in his chair, grabbed his own binoculars, and peered through them. "Some of our guests will be thrilled," he said and pressed the ship-wide intercom button on the console of his chair to make the announcement.

He stood and paced around his chair, going over the same thoughts. It was an angry loop that he couldn't seem to stop. *I made the right decision. Why can't I believe that? They're all the same.* He clenched his teeth. *She wants everything her way and is unwilling to see my side of it. Her career. Her family. Her friends. What about me? I'm willing to give up a lot for her. I only want to be with her and no other woman, but she can't see that. I'd buy her a mansion for us to live in and raise our family. We would have a wonderful life on the sea and in San Diego. She could design her clothes, and we could have a family and still be here on the ship. She could visit her family, and they could come visit us.*

He left the bridge and walked into his cabin. Picking up the phone, he called the manager of the jewelry department. "This is Captain DiMarco. I'd like you to come to my cabin with a selection of engagement rings. Nothing smaller than three carats... Don't forget to include the emerald and diamond *Toi et Moi ring* you have on display in the window."

DINNER HAD ENDED, and some guests dressed in their finest formal attire strolled around the decks, while others went to the various lounges. The atrium served as a ballroom just as it had for the Captain's cocktail party and all the other formal events. It had been set up for dancing. The fifteen piece orchestra played slow romantic music. Men in tuxedos and women in beautiful gowns whirled on the dance floor.

Some of the guests nodded to Lorenzo as he walked in. He saw her dressed in a red, strapless silk mermaid gown that hugged the curves of her body. From her rounded hips, the dress was covered in red silk rosettes. Her blond hair was pulled away from her face and flowing in waves around her shoulders and down her bare back.

He was about to do something he *never* did. Lorenzo nodded to the orchestra leader, and the music stopped. A hush fell over the crowd. He'd foregone the receiving line. One of his officers nudged another one. Lorenzo smiled to himself. *No one would win the bet tonight. No, Captain's specials would be delivered to any of the women tomorrow.*

The chords of the waltz he requested began to play. "May I have this dance?"

His sexy voice sent heat sizzling through her body. Francesca stood there, eyes wide. He dominated the room and she couldn't believe that he asked her to dance. He never danced with the guests. They'd only danced in his cabin. She gazed into Lorenzo's black eyes. Eyes that she'd gotten lost in over and over again while they made love.

Lorenzo bowed to her. And she curtsied before she placed her hand in his warm, large hand.

"You look beautiful," he said, kissing the knuckles of her hand before his fingers curled around hers.

She was too surprised to say anything. The waltz was familiar to her. *How long will I love you*, began. The room melted away, and there was only him. Oh, so handsome. His broad shoulders and his athletic frame encased in his formal captain's uniform. His scent drifted around her. Even in her gold stiletto heels the top of her head just about reached under his chin. She couldn't talk. She moved into his arms, happy to be held in his powerful embrace.. She tipped her head up. "I thought you said that you don't dance at these events."

"I'm making an exception for you, Imp." His husky whisper sent tingles through her body.

He spun her around in the steps of the waltz. "I miss holding you in my arms."

"Don't say things you don't mean."

"I've never lied to you, Francesca. I miss you."

The music ended, and Francesca listened to the round of applause. She felt her cheeks flame, but her dashing sea captain was calm and, as always, in charge. He bent over her hand, kissing the knuckles, then he entwined his fingers with hers, and they left the dance floor.

"If we hurry, no one will know we're gone."

She didn't say anything. She just held his hand, and they walked over to the officer's elevator. Her heart fluttered.

"Will you have a cocktail with me?"

"Yes, I will."

The elevator doors silently slid open, and they walked the few steps into Lorenzo's cabin. He went to the bar. "Champagne?"

"Yes, please." She followed him over. He lifted the bottle from a silver ice bucket and popped the cork. Lorenzo poured some into the two crystal flutes sitting on the bar. Taking one, he handed it to Francesca. They touched rims in a silent toast before they sipped the icy cold sparkling wine.

"Come sit on the sofa with me. I have something I need to say to you… I'm going to call Ricardo. *Tesoro mio*, I'll go back to Palermo take the position of COO. I want to do this for you, Francesca. I love you more than anything else. You are everything to me."

"No. I was selfish. I don't want you to do something you really don't want to do."

"Tesoro..." He moved off the couch and dropped down on one knee.

Lorenzo reached into his jacket pocket and removed a black velvet box. He lifted the lid and placed the box on the coffee table. He held out a *Toi et Moi* ring. The you and me ring was set with a round diamond and square emerald. Clear diamond baguette stones were set on both shanks.

She gasped, "Zo."

"Francesca Russo, *Tesoro mio.* I love you and want you to be happy. I want to spend the rest of my life making you happy. Will you marry me?"

Tears filled her eyes and streamed down her cheeks. "Oh Zo, yes, I will marry you. You don't have to go back to Palermo. I was self-centered, selfish... and so wrong. I will be happy wherever you are. You are *everything* to me." He slipped the exquisite *you and me* ring on her finger.

"A perfect fit," she said admiring the ring.

He stood, taking her in his arms. "Yes *Tesoro* we are. I want to talk to your parents, and Gus...we can fly back to Palermo after we dock in San Diego. My brother can send one of DiMarco Enterprises private jets for us."

She lifted her hands to his broad shoulders. "But what about the rest of your time working? Don't you have another six or so weeks?"

"No worries, Imp. There is always an emergency captain on board. She can take charge. We have a wedding to plan. I have a palazzo in Palermo given to me from my mother's family. It belonged to my great, great, great grandmother, the Contessa Rinaldi. It will need some renovating, updating to modernize the electrical and plumbing, but it will be a fabulous home for you and me to raise a family. We can buy a place to live in while we have the work done."

"Zo, that sounds wonderful and we can do all that. But right now, help me get out of this dress and make love to me."

"Amore, ti ammo," he said before taking her mouth with his.

~

THANK you for reading THE SEA CAPTAIN'S REDEMPTION. I hope you enjoyed Francesca and Lorenzo's love story.

Are you longing for more? Then come lose yourself in

A ROYAL TEMPTATION

KINDERGARTEN TEACHER SARINA MOORE is desperate for money. A dream job aboard a luxury yacht cruising the Mediterranean will provide that. Her excitement is shattered when she realizes the position is not what she agreed to.

Sarina must escape the *Carmella* before it sets sail.

Jason Donato was born to wealth and privilege he is accustomed to getting whatever he desires. His every command is immediately obeyed.

Right now, he desires the temptingly beautiful red head Sarina Moore. Keeping his true identity from her he offers her shelter. Her innocent abandon ignites a fire that scorches his soul, but all he will offer her is sex the way he likes it. With no strings, no commitments, and no promises. Can Sarina have a happily ever after on those terms?

A Royal Temptation

WHERE TO FIND MY BOOKS

You can find my books at your favorite bookstore, retailer, or library 📚

Or, you can buy them directly from me at my website https:// CindyReddingAuthor.com

Or,

Cindy's Store https://payhip.com/CindyRedding

If you prefer, please scan this QR Code with your phone

ABOUT THE AUTHOR

USA TODAY Bestselling Author **Cindy Redding** writes what she loves. Contemporary sizzling hot and spicy romance. Inspired by her travels around the world and her love of Italy, Cindy's romances come alive with hot-blooded heroes and strong-willed independent heroines. Escape to a world where happily ever after lives.

Sign up for my newsletter and receive THE TYCOON'S SECRET CHILD as my FREE gift to you. Happy Reading!

The Tycoon's Secret Child

ALSO BY CINDY REDDING

The DiMarco Empire Series

The Sicilian's Betrayal

The Winemaker's Seduction

The Frenchman's Revenge

Christmas

A Fake Date for Kate

The Christmas Present

The Royals

A Royal Temptation

More Billionaire Romances

The Tycoon's Secret Child

ACKNOWLEDGMENTS

I would like to thank Heather Starling for all of her invaluable advice and wonderful insight. I want to especially thank SJS Editorial Services for their quick and thorough editing. You make me shine.

www.ingramcontent.com/pod-product-compliance
Lightning Source LLC
Chambersburg PA
CBHW020116310726
48970CB00002B/663